The
Quietness

The
Quietness

Alison Rattle

HOT
KEY
BOOKS

First published in Great Britain in 2013 by Hot Key Books
Northburgh House, 10 Northburgh Street, London EC1V 0AT

A CIP catalogue record for this book is available from the British Library.

ISBN: 978-1-4714-0101-5

2

Typeset by Palimpsest Book Production Limited, Falkirk, Stirlingshire
This book is set in 10.5pt Berling LT Std

Printed and bound by Clays Ltd, St Ives Plc

FSC

Hot Key Books supports the Forest Stewardship Council (FSC), the leading
international forest certification organisation, and is committed to printing
only on Greenpeace-approved FSC-certified paper.

www.hotkeybooks.com

Hot Key Books is part of the Bonnier Publishing Group
www.bonnierpublishing.com

For my wonderful children, Daisy, Ella and Riley. Remember it's never too late to chase your dreams! And for my Paul. Love you everything. X9

London
January, 1870

1

Queenie

It was a wet day. The rain had turned the roads to sludge. Everyone unlucky enough to be out on the streets hurried past Queenie, without even glancing at the heap of fruit she'd polished to gleaming on her skirts. No matter how hard she shouted, 'PENNY A LOT, FINE RUSSETS!' or, 'EIGHT A PENNY, STUNNING PEARS!'

It was the worst of days. Queenie and Da had been shouting themselves hoarse for hours; Da with his tray of apples strung around his neck and Queenie with a basket of pears balanced on her head. On good days they could easily take two shillings and Mam would buy a bit of bacon and butter to have with their bread, and sometimes they'd have taters, roasted crisp in the fire. But today was different. They hadn't even made enough pennies for a hot pie and a glass of beer.

Da swore under his breath, 'Sod this for a trade. How's a man to wet his bleedin' throat?' His face had turned red and Queenie knew his temper would soon be flaring. 'Come on, my gal,' he suddenly shouted. 'If the beggars won't come to us, we'll go to them.'

Queenie followed Da down winding alleys while the clouds spilt their innards. The rain had loosened the mud

3

and set free all manner of frights to float down the road. Turds, broken plates and bits of dead dog swirled around her ankles. They stopped outside the gin-shop. A darker, more evil-smelling place Queenie couldn't imagine. It crouched low on the corner of the road. Its two grimy windows, hung with cobwebs and tattered curtains, were like a pair of blinking eyes staring out at her. She knew she had to go inside or there would be a beating from Da and the taste of blood in her mouth. But it made her guts twist in fright to think of it. It was no good staying on the streets, though. So she lifted up her apron, filled it with pears and pushed open the door with her shoulder.

The room inside was long and low, the floorboards rotten and covered with dirty remains of straw. The air was thick with tobacco smoke and the sour smell of vomit. Customers crowded around the bar drinking; painted women groaned and cursed, and men with red, bloated faces and beady eyes reached out their hands to grab at her flesh.

'*Here's a pretty one ripe for the plucking,*' said a voice.

Hot breath so close she could taste it.

'*Over here, missy. A penny for a kiss and a feel of your arse.*'

A shiny brown penny was lying on the floor. As Queenie bent to pick it up, stubby fingers found their way up her skirt and prodded at her where they shouldn't. The pears fell from her apron, but the penny was warm in her hand. She stood up and looked around at the leering faces.

'A PENNY FOR A FEEL OF A RIPE, JUICY ARSE!' she

shouted, and ten minutes later she was back on the street with a handful of coins and the rain cooling the burning of her cheeks.

Back home, when Mam's face lit up at the sound of coins jingling in her apron pocket, Queenie thought of the groping fingers and how easy it had been to collect a fistful of fat pennies. But as she ate bread still warm and doughy from the baker's, Queenie could feel the throb of bruises between her legs. She felt deep down dirty. A new kind of dirty that didn't feel right. She swore she would never let Da force her into one of those places again. She would rather starve. Or take a belting.

Queenie looked around the pokey room she shared with Mam, Da, the little ones and the baby. Seven of them in one room. Seven empty bellies to fill. The little ones like scrawny fledglings with their throats always open, begging for food; crying for a mouthful of sweet bread or the taste of warm fresh milk. There were seven of them to huddle round the stove now that Da had managed to set a meagre fire burning.

'Fit to warm the backside of 'er Majesty the Queen,' he pronounced, all la-di-da.

They all sat close; the hot licks of flames brought a blush to the little ones' sunken cheeks and chased the cold from Queenie's aching bones. Mam set the tea kettle to boil and when the spurts of steam sailed from the broken spout, Queenie thought of the black funnels of the trains at Waterloo spewing out big, soft feather pillows. She could almost smell the excitement, the oily scent of travel; people

5

arriving and people leaving. She imagined boarding one of those trains one day, carrying a fine leather suitcase and wearing a fancy bonnet, perhaps, and a velvet-trimmed dress. Just like the well-to-do-ladies who sometimes threw a coin from the window of their carriages as they flew by; wheels and horses' hooves churning up the mud on Blackfriars Road. Queenie could always imagine leaving, but she could never imagine where her journey would end.

Mam handed round mugs of hot water with a spit of tea from the weekly dregs and pulled out her titty from the top of her dress to feed the baby. Mam was forever talking. Klattering on and on, Da would say, speaking so nicely, turning each word out carefully. Like she'd got a mouthful of plums. A mouthful of fat, purple, juicy plums.

'On account of 'er livin' with them swanks,' Da would tease. 'Got to 'er just in time, I did. Afore she was spoilt goods.' He'd wink at Queenie but Mam's face would close up and her klattering would stop, at least until Da had whispered something in her ear and kissed her hard on the lips.

Mam was going on now, telling Da how Gaffy from up the top had gone for his missus again and knocked out the last of her teeth. The little ones were squawking and fighting over a crust of bread.

Queenie closed her eyes and tried to be somewhere else. Anywhere else than in the dingy room she called home; such a dark, damp place, hidden down a passageway in the tangle of streets between Waterloo and London Bridge.

The houses were so close together they held each other up. There was no room for the sun to shine down and dry out the wet filth that trickled down the walls and ran through the gutters in front of each doorway. Broken windows were stuffed with brown paper, stinking pools overflowed with shit and slops were emptied from windows. A foul stench hung in the air, clung to clothes and seeped so deep into her skin that Queenie never knew what clean smelt like.

There were bodies everywhere. Men, women and the ghosts of children. The men lounged in doorways, leaned from windows, or slept where they fell drunk in the gutter. There was laughter and wailing, fighting and dirty words. Shouting and squabbling, drinking and smoking. Hollow moans late at night.

Queenie could hear it all now. There was never any quiet with families crowded into every room. Gaffy the cobbler on the first floor, chestnut roasters on the second and Dirty Sal in the back room with her five screaming nippers.

'Penny for your thoughts, my big gal,' said Da.

Queenie opened her eyes and looked at him grinning at her, with his arm around Mam's shoulder, sitting there as though he was lord of the manor. Like Mam and the little ones and a belly full of bread and beer were all he needed in the world to be happy.

'I ain't telling you,' she said. 'They're just my thoughts. They belong to me.'

And before Da could say anything else she went to the corner of the room, wrapped her shawl tight around herself and lay down on the pile of straw she shared as a bed with her brothers.

'Tomorrow,' she promised herself. 'Tomorrow will be different.'

She closed her eyes and wished and wished for some quietness.

2

Ellen

'Mary, not so tight!' I gasped, as she pulled the laces at the back of my corset. It was a miserable morning, the skies covered in a curtain of fog. The fire that Mary had lit in my bedroom was failing to chase away the cruel, icy draughts that crept through the floorboards and window frames. My arms were dotted in goosebumps and the fresh petticoat that Mary had laid out on the bed for me was already dirtied by a thin layer of greasy soot that had blown down the chimney.

My stomach hurt. The cramps which accompanied my monthly bleed pulled at my insides and the bones in my corset poked spitefully in my ribs. The bell for breakfast rang and I nudged Mary.

'It's tight enough, I think. Now hurry with my hair.' Father couldn't bear anyone to be late to the table and I did not want to draw on his displeasure. I did not want the morning to be made any more miserable.

The rag I had bloodied in the night was in a dish on my dressing table. Mary finished arranging my hair and covered the dish with a cloth ready to carry it downstairs to Father. He would glance at the contents and make a note in his diary. Then Mary would be dismissed down to the kitchen where she would burn the crimson-stained rag on the fire.

It had always been this way; since that first shocking morning in my twelfth year when I had woken to a dull ache in my back and a slipperiness between my thighs. The blood had soaked through my nightgown and left islands of red on my sheets. I knew it had come from deep inside me and I knew I was dying. It was Mary who found me kneeling by the bed, shivering in terror as I prayed for my life. It was Mary who calmed me and cleaned me with warm, wet cloths and told me I was 'certainly not dying', but had merely become a woman. She sat me in my armchair and wrapped me in a shawl and, as she pulled the soiled sheets from the bed and rolled them up, she told me she must inform Father of the event; that he had instructed her to tell him when it happened and that she dared not disobey him no matter how I cried and begged her not to.

Every month since then, I have prayed for the blood not to arrive. Prayed not to feel that weight of shame and hatred when I picture Father examining my dirty secret. Father places great importance on the regularity of a girl's monthly bleed.

'It is my duty as your father to see that your menstrual flow is observed with care. Any irregularities can only lead to hysteria, or, in the very worst of cases – insanity.'

Father knows all this because he is an anatomist. An *eminent* anatomist. He takes his carriage most days to the University College Hospital where he studies the workings of the human body. He has published a book on his findings: *Swift's Compendium of Anatomy*. It is a work of great importance. Bound in polished brown leather, its pages are heavy with the secrets of the dead.

On a warm day last spring, not long after I had turned fifteen, Father told me to dress for an outing in his carriage.

'It is time you were introduced to the world,' he said.

Mary had been beside herself with excitement and persuaded me to dab some rouge on my cheeks.

'He's sure to be taking you to Rotten Row, miss. A ride around Hyde Park to show you off to the gentlemen of town. He'll be wanting to find you a husband. You mark my words!' She squealed with delight as she bustled around me fixing my hair and smoothing my skirts. Could it be true? I did not dare to hope so. But I remember I felt as though I was floating and my heart was beating fast, like the heart of a frightened mouse.

Father did not take me to Hyde Park. Father took me to the hospital. He took me down into the dirty yellow light of the dissecting room. Lying on a table was a man. His head was shaven; his skin brown and papery. I stood as though in a trance. Father walked towards the body and picked up a scalpel. I could not look away. He used the scalpel to slice down the centre of the body. Then he pulled it apart and dipped his hands inside. A hot stench of vile sweetness filled my nostrils and my breakfast rose in my throat.

'Do you have any questions?' asked Father.

I was dizzy and weak. From behind my lace handkerchief, I managed to ask Father who the man had been.

'No one of consequence,' he replied. 'Just an unclaimed wretch from the asylum.'

I must have fainted then, for I awoke back in the carriage with a damp handkerchief on my forehead. Father was staring at me.

'It is a pity you were not born a boy,' he said. 'You would have appreciated the great service I am doing mankind and be inspired to carry on my good works. As it is, it is enough that you saw it with your own eyes.'

I think Father knows all there is to know about the inner workings of the human body. He knows people from the inside out. I think that was what he was trying to tell me in the sadness of that yellow room. That he knows inside of me. He knows all of me and I can never hide from him.

As soon as Mary had finished my hair, I hurried downstairs to the dining room. Mother was already sitting at the table. She is a wisp of a woman, so pale and fragile that I sometimes think the merest breath of wind could carry her over the rooftops of London and lay her to sleep on a cloud. She was dressed as usual in black silk, trimmed with stiff crepe, her silver hair hidden under a lace cap. I have never known her to wear anything other than black. All my life Mother has been in mourning for her dead babies.

'Never able to keep one,' Mary told me once. 'All of 'em dead before they came out. Poor woman.' I had looked at her, puzzled, and she had looked back at me with a faraway look in her eyes before suddenly seeing my face.

'Well, 'cept for you, of course. She was allowed to keep you.'

I often think those dead babies must have taken her love away with them. Bit by bit, one by one, until by the time I came along there was none left for me.

Mother barely nodded her head as I whispered her a good morning. We sat in silence, listening to the shouts of the newspaper boy and the double beat of horses' hooves that rattled along the road outside. Ninny, the cook, and Mary came into the room and waited at the back for morning prayers to be said. Mary had changed into a clean apron ready to serve breakfast but Ninny had grease spots and smears of bacon fat on her bib. I could hear her breath whistling loudly through her nostrils. She shuffled and sniffed and wiped the sweat from her top lip with the back of her hand.

The dining room door opened at last and Father walked in to take his place at the head of the table. The room held its breath, and even Ninny's nose-whistling paused, as Father looked at us all with his watery eyes and then bent his head to pray.

Every day it is the same. Ninny retreats from the room as Father's *Amen* settles in the air like the soot on the mantelpiece. Mary pours the tea and serves the muffins and bacon, while we, the eminent anatomist Dr William Walter Swift, his wife Eliza and I, their daughter Ellen, sit like strangers.

Mother will eat barely a bite before excusing herself and evaporating from the room as though she was never there. She hates the world outside her bedroom. She sits in there day after day, surrounded by fresh flowers and her cages of birds: her finches, parakeets and golden canaries. Her little 'sugar birds'. I sometimes think she is half bird herself, with her brittle bones and beady eyes.

Father has a hearty appetite, and will eat a whole plate

of bacon and a pile of greasy muffins before he folds his newspaper in half and takes out his pocket watch. At precisely half past nine he places the watch back in his pocket and calls for his coat and hat. The front door slams behind him and the ornaments on the sideboard rattle in agitation before the vibrations settle and the house sighs in relief. Then I am left alone in the quietness, with nothing but my books and my dreams of finding love and the emptiness of the day stretching before me.

Except that on this particular morning, Father made an announcement and I somehow knew that my life would never be the same again.

3

Queenie

Queenie was woken by a low moaning noise. She opened her eyes. It was morning, and from her straw bed by the far wall, Queenie could see the baby lying still on the floor, his thin blanket rucked around his middle so his little legs poked out, all dry and bent like twigs. Mam was sitting slumped on the edge of her and Da's bed, her mouth wide open, and her arms dangling.

Da roared, 'Shut up, will you!' and Queenie saw him sitting in the corner of the room, rocking back on his heels. He had that same hard look in his eyes as when he'd been on the beer, and he'd taken his prized neckerchief off and was twisting it round and round in his fingers.

'Is the baby dead?' asked Queenie.

Mam started to moan louder. The sound maddened Queenie and she wanted to tell Mam to shut up too. Babies came and went all the time. It had been a weak little scrap anyway, always whining for the titty. And Queenie knew there was another one on the way. There always was. Da had got into the habit of passing Mam his portion of bread again and her cotton gown was pulling tight across her belly. Queenie wanted to ask them why the devil they brought any of them into the world when there was never enough money for them to eat proper, let alone enjoy themselves. But she didn't. Not with Da in that mood. She just stayed on the straw and let the little ones press close to her.

Da wouldn't look up from the floor, like it was his fault the baby had died. Queenie watched as he stood and gathered the baby up with quick angry movements and parcelled it in the blanket. Without his neckerchief tied at his throat, Da looked unfinished. The green silk with its yellow flowers belonged around Da's neck and not in his hands. It told the world who he was: a seller of fruit and vegetables. A costermonger. He was so proud of his green silk; it was a bad thing that he'd taken it off. He'd be taking it to the pawnshop, Queenie knew. Hoping for a few shillings to bury the baby. He didn't try to comfort Mam or even kiss her before he slammed out the door.

After he'd gone, the room seemed smaller. Mam had finally shut up and was lying down on her bed with her face to the wall. The little ones were tugging at Queenie and wailing for their breakfast. She shook them off and they straight away hunched together again: a pile of wide eyes and jutting bones. Queenie could hardly tell who was who any more. Which was Tally? Which was Kit? Which was Albie? They were all of them shrunk to skin and bone with tatty hair and smudged-out faces. Queenie couldn't bear to look at them or to watch Mam lying there with her arms all empty. Besides, hunger was growling around her insides like a mad dog on the loose.

There'd be nothing to sell today, Queenie knew that. No spare shillings to buy pears from the market to fill her basket, not with a burial to pay for now. But she couldn't stand to stay in the sadness of that room, not when there were other ways of cadging a penny or two; plenty of other ways.

Outside, great slabs of fog, the colour of dirty linen, hung in the passageways as she trailed her fingers along the walls of houses to find her way out on to the streets. The fog was always bad here, being so close to the river, and the lingering smells it brought with it were enough to make a cat retch. But Queenie never minded it. She liked to disappear in it; it made her feel free somehow, and made for easy pickings if you were of a mind to relieve a careless gentleman of his purse.

She would walk to Waterloo Bridge, she decided; there were always plenty of people about there. By midday the fog turned a murky yellow, and she liked to stand on the bridge and watch how the tall chimneys of factories and the bulky warehouses on the banks of the river got blurred in the greasy veil and were turned into mysterious golden palaces.

There would only be six of them now, she thought, living in their pokey little room. One less mouth to feed. And she felt lighter somehow, and unbuttoned and easy, and she even noticed a faint tongue of sunlight licking its way through the fog. Just the sight of it warmed her insides.

4

Ellen

Mother had just taken a tiny bite of her muffin when Father loudly cleared his throat. The crumb, which had been balancing delicately between Mother's front teeth, shot out across the table and lay quivering in the centre of the white lace tablecloth. Mother clamped her napkin to her mouth in horror and we both looked across at Father.

He had not touched his breakfast and was already folding his newspaper. Mary had set a candle on the table next to him. The flicker of the flame and the grey morning light had given his face the waxy complexion of a corpse. Flesh hung from under his eyes and mutton-chop whiskers grew wide and long on the broad sides of his head. His hands were slender, though, despite his fatness; his fingers long and tapering and delicate like a woman's. They made me shudder.

Father cleared his throat again. He used words sparingly. Mealtimes were for nourishing the body and not for idle chatter. His deliveries of the morning prayers were the only words ever permitted to break the silence of the dining room.

'I received a letter this morning,' he stated, and he took a fold of paper from his pocket and slowly spread it out.

He had never addressed us at the meal table before and I had to hold my hands in my lap to stop them from trembling.

'It seems,' said Father, 'that my dear sister Isabella is no longer with us.' He scanned the letter again. 'Ah, yes. Thrown from her carriage and trampled upon by horses.'

There was a gasp from Mother and she clutched at her throat. Mary hurried to her side and poured her a glass of water.

'Yes,' continued Father. 'It would seem she met her end in a most ghastly fashion.'

My mind was racing. Who was Isabella? I had no idea that Father had a sister. Questions bubbled into my mouth, one on top of the other. Questions I knew I could not ask now.

'However,' said Father, 'I will spare you further details. All you need know is that her sixteen-year-old son, Jacob Grey, will be coming to stay with us for a time.'

A cousin, I thought. I have a cousin?

There was a thud and a clatter of cutlery. I turned to find Mother had fainted. I sighed. She would be indisposed for days now, and I would have to attend to her birds as she sipped her tonics and twittered out instructions from the depths of her bed.

'So,' said Father. He folded the letter carefully, ignoring Mother's predicament. 'It seems we must extend our hospitality to this . . . boy. It would not do to be seen as uncharitable. Mary, you will get the blue room ready for our guest. And, from tomorrow, this household will be in mourning. Now, fetch my hat and coat and clean up

19

this . . . mess.' He waved his arm over the table at the leftover remains of breakfast and at Mother, spilt across the table like a jug of milk.

The front door slammed and Mary *tsk-tsked* as she helped Mother from her chair. I did not offer to assist. I was thinking of Isabella Grey, of an aunt I had not known existed, and of Jacob Grey. My cousin, Jacob Grey. I liked the name. *Jacob Grey, Jacob Grey*, I whispered. It tasted good, like a bowl of spiced soup on a cold wet day, or the crisp skin of pork, salty and hot from the fire. Would he be handsome? I wondered. Would he be kind? What would he think of me? He would be grieving, I reminded myself. I hoped I could offer him some comfort.

5

Queenie

It had been three days since the baby died and Da was still not home. Queenie sat on the musty straw in the corner of the room shivering. The little ones were sleeping next to her, and Mam still hadn't moved off her bed. Mam had done nothing but sleep or stare at the walls. She'd stopped sobbing at least and the little ones had stopped mithering, but the quietness was the wrong sort.

Da would be drinking, Queenie knew, but he'd never stayed away for this long before. Sometimes when he didn't come home all night Mam would send her out in the morning chill to search the streets and gin-shops. She'd peer down dim alleyways and into doorways, hoping like mad that one of the lumps sleeping under their jackets would be Da; his pockets empty and his breath stinking of stale beer. She'd pray to catch a glimpse of the green and yellow of his neckerchief, bright against the stubble on his face. Often as not she'd find him curled under a table, snoring gently into the early morning silence of a gin-shop; an empty mug still held in his hand and a pack of cards scattered across the table. After she'd shaken him awake, they would hold tight to each other as she steered him through the streets back home.

But it had been three whole days, and she'd run out of places to look. There was only the workhouse now, or Horsemonger Lane Gaol, and she hoped he wasn't in either of those places. People never came out of those dark holes.

Queenie hadn't fared too well out on the streets the last few days. She'd managed to snatch a hot pie from a street vendor, and to hide herself quickly while his angry hollers got swallowed up in the fog. But then a quick-witted gentleman had smashed her leg with his walking stick when he felt her hand creep into his coat pocket. Now Queenie was bruised and sore and knew she wouldn't be able to outrun a swift stranger.

Queenie got up from the pile of straw and limped over to the bed. 'Mam,' she said, 'Mam! Get up now. Come on. The little 'uns are starving. We need you. Come on!'

It was Mam, but not Mam, who eventually turned to look at her. It was Mam's face, but there was something wrong with her eyes. They were flat and dead like the glassy eyes of the bloaters down at Billingsgate.

'I've looked all over for Da,' said Queenie. 'I can't find him nowhere. Maybe he ain't coming back this time.' She shook Mam's shoulder hard. 'Come on! You need to get up now!'

Mam sighed deeply and slowly rose from the bed. She stood up and began to tidy herself. Queenie watched her scrape her fingers through her hair and wash her face with spit on a rag. Her hair was black and velvety. Da always said it was like a dark summer's night. When she unpinned it a shower of dust flew out, and curls rolled down her back stopping just short of her waist. Da was mad for her hair. He would take a thick length and bury his face in the depths of it and cry out, 'Thank you, Lord, for my own sweet Dollymop!'

Mam would push him away and tell him to keep his filthy hands to himself, but her eyes would be laughing as she tied her hair back into place. But Da wasn't here now and Mam wasn't laughing.

'Mam,' Queenie said. 'How're we going to eat? There's no money to go to market. Why's Da buggered off again? Don't he care a bit?'

'Your Da's a proud man,' said Mam quietly, like she was talking to herself. 'With the baby gone and that . . . he thinks he's failed us. But I'm *not* proud, and I won't see another of my children starve.'

She hung a sheet across the middle of the room and told Queenie to keep the little ones quiet. It wasn't hard. They barely murmured when she pulled them close and whispered them stories of talking rats and hidden treasures. Tally, the eldest, was learning his letters and Queenie helped him to shape them using a stick to scrape in the dirt floor. Soon the little ones grew tired and drifted off to sleep curled up tight to each other.

Mam was in and out all that day, bringing strange men with her, one at a time, into the room. Queenie never saw them, only heard them as they wheezed through the door and dropped their trousers on the floor. They didn't speak much, just grunted and sniffed or coughed and spat. Some of them banged the bed against the wall for an age, but others only took a minute to let out a groan of satisfaction,

23

like they'd dined on a plate of good roast beef and couldn't eat another morsel. Mam didn't sigh like she did when she was with Da. She hardly made a sound; only cried out a couple of times like she was hurting.

Queenie knew what she was doing and thought of the bloated faces in the gin-shop and grubby fingers fumbling beneath her own skirts. She was glad it was Mam this time.

Mam was quiet a long time after the last of the men had paid up and left. Queenie fell asleep and dreamt of fat pigs gobbling up troughs of plums and Da spinning Mam around the room, faster and faster, her hair flying across her face and Da laughing and laughing.

'Queenie, Queenie . . . come on, now. Quick. Take this.' Mam was shaking her awake and pressing coins into her hand. 'Go on now and fetch some coal. And some bread and dripping. Oh, and best get a pennyworth of tea while you're at it.' She'd taken the sheet down and pinned her hair back up. Queenie grabbed the coins and hurried towards the door. She glimpsed a man's felt cap lying on the floor beside the roughed-up bed and wondered for a moment how Da would feel about his space being borrowed by dirty strangers. He could think what he bleedin' well liked, she decided. He'd be here if he cared that much.

They had the finest meal in all of London that night. Mam made the tea strong and hot and she covered door-steps of bread in a thick layer of white dripping that tasted like heaven. They ate until their lips and cheeks were shiny with grease. The coals in the stove turned ashen and Mam began to sing softly to herself as she stroked her mound of belly.

> *Cry baby bunting*
> *Daddy's gone a-hunting*
> *Gone to fetch a rabbit skin*
> *To wrap the baby bunting in.*

6

Ellen

Mary had finished putting Mother back to bed and was airing the blue guest room and removing dust sheets. I walked past her and along the corridor to Mother's room. It was dark inside. The curtains were drawn and the air was musty with the sour odour of bird droppings. My eyes adjusted to the light and I saw the small hump of Mother lying in the centre of her bed, the covers drawn up to her chin.

'Is that you, Mary?' she whispered. 'Fetch me my shawl.'

'No, Mother, it is me,' I said. 'It is Ellen.'

'What do you want, girl?' she hissed. 'Go and get Mary for me.'

'I just want to talk to you for a moment,' I said. 'Where is your shawl? I will fetch it for you.'

'Talk?' she said. 'Talk? Can you not see I am indisposed? Get Mary now.'

'But Mother, it will only take a moment. I want to ask you about Aunt Isabella, and . . . and Jacob Grey.'

'How dare you!' she spluttered. 'This has nothing to do with you. Now leave me in peace.'

'But I have an aunt I know nothing about! And a cousin! Why have they never been spoken of before?'

Mother coughed; dry little barks, and she waved me away with her hand.

'Get me Mary,' she croaked.

'But Mother,' I persisted, 'I have a right to know about my family!'

'You,' she whispered, seemingly exhausted from her coughing, 'have no right to know anything. Now fetch Mary!'

She closed her eyes and I knew it was of no use to ask again. What was wrong with me that she could not love me? I swallowed hard to hold back my tears and left the room, daring to close the door hard behind me. Mother's birds started squawking and flapping and I thought that even though they were caged, at least they were loved.

I hurried back to the guest room where Mary was smoothing the counterpane on the newly made-up bed.

'Mother is asking for you,' I told her. She turned to go and I put my hand on her arm to stop her. 'Mary. What can you tell me of my Aunt Isabella and my cousin?' I felt her stiffen under my touch.

'I . . . I . . . I don't truly know, miss,' she said. 'I think it best that you don't ask me.'

'Do not be silly, Mary, what is there to hide? I will find out soon enough. Jacob Grey will be here in a few days.'

'I know, miss, but it's something that's never spoken of. It is a family matter and I don't wish to lose my position by talking out of turn.'

'That would never happen,' I said. 'Please, just tell me what you know.'

'Miss,' she sighed, 'all I know is there were words between

27

your father and his sister. Harsh words, and many years ago. Her name has never been spoken since. Now let me get on and don't you breathe a word.'

I nodded and let go of her arm. She walked briskly out of the room. I watched her go and wondered what I would ever do without her. When all the governesses came and went over the years, the cold, distant women who taught me my letters and how to keep quiet, Mary was my only comfort. She laughed at my attempts to speak French, smuggled pieces of cake to my room and listened to me as I read her passages from my favourite books.

'You'll be the most beautiful bride in London one of these days, miss,' she told me as she brushed my hair at bedtimes.

'Will my husband be handsome?' I asked her. 'And will he be rich?'

'But of course, miss, he'll be the most handsome, richest man ever.'

'And will we have children?'

'Hoards of 'em,' she said with a wink.

'Then you will have to come and live with us, won't you? To look after us all.'

'That I will, miss, that I will,' she would say.

I looked around the guest room: at the new cake of soap on the wash stand and the plumped-up pillows on the bed. I hoped the days would pass quickly and that Jacob Grey would arrive safely.

7

Queenie

For as long as Queenie could remember, Mam had told stories. If she couldn't feed Queenie's belly with tasty morsels, she would fill her head instead. Mam's words took Queenie to warm places where there was always a fire burning and a table laden with food. She told of the taste of hot winter broths and steaming apple pies. Her words filled Queenie's empty spaces and took away the sharp gnaw of hunger. As the little ones came along, first Tally, then Kit, then Albie, Mam made room for them all in the rough folds of her skirts as they sat by her feet and listened hard. Da was never there. He was always out on the beer. 'He'll be home soon,' Mam would say hopefully. 'With a rabbit for the pot maybe, and a blanket for the next baby.'

Queenie loved Mam telling of the time before she met Da. In the days when she was young and pretty and worked in a house on the other side of the river. In a house that was as white as the bone on a newly boiled ham, she said. The house was full of rooms. So many rooms, there were doors that were never opened. It smelt of warm honey; of polished rosewood and hair oil; cigar smoke and lavender. Queenie could only imagine those smells, but they sounded good enough to eat. Every space was filled with dark furniture that was covered by lace. There was even paper on the walls with patterns of birds, flowers and ivy coloured in reds and greens and golds.

Then Mam would tell of the room full of books. Floor to ceiling full of books. The grandest books you ever saw; smart in leather bindings and all tucked neatly into their own little space on a shelf. Mam dusted those books, one by one. Ever so careful. Queenie imagined what an age it must have taken. Hundreds of them, there was. Sometimes, Mam whispered, she would dare to pick up the books and open the covers to smell the ink. She liked to feel the paper between her fingers. Some pages felt rough and heavy but others felt as light as onion skins. Best of all were the pictures hidden between the pages: flowers in all their detail, dark-skinned men in strange costumes, beautiful ladies dressed like ships in full sail and the most curious of creatures. Great birds the colour of jewels with beaks as long as swords, and monsters with claws and horns as thick as your legs. It was in that room that Mam learned her letters. With all those books, she said, she couldn't help herself.

Once, Mam said, she found a book so foul she could scarce imagine the mind that had thought of it! Full of drawings of sharp knives and peculiar instruments and of men's bodies laid out on butcher's blocks and all cut open so the insides were on view to the world. And words so long she couldn't make head nor tail of them. Mam said the books only got half a dusting that day and she felt as green as a quarter of soap right up till bedtime.

Mam would tell how she lit fires, swept ashes, scrubbed

floors, brushed carpets, beat rugs and cleaned walls. The paper on the walls was so beautiful it couldn't be allowed to get dirty. With the fires going all day, the soot settled on the paper and hid the colours. So Mam blew off the dust from top to bottom with a pair of bellows. Then she got a loaf of bread and broke it in half. She wiped the bread over the paper. Not too hard, or else the dirt stuck and never came off and the paper was ruined. So bit by bit Mam rubbed the loaf gently down the walls and the crumbs collected the dirt and the whole lot fell to the floor to be swept up tidily.

As Queenie got older she grew tired of Mam's stories. She got angry at the picture in her head of bread being broken to wipe away soot. Bread that could fill bellies being crumbled and wasted and swept up with the dirt. But as the feeling inside her grew she knew it wasn't anger after all. It was bigger than anger and stronger and she realised she didn't mind about the bread. She didn't care. Not one bit. She just wanted to live in that fancy house, to be just like those fancy people and to have her own walls to cover in fancy paper. She wanted to have great baskets of bread delivered to her fancy door every day. Baskets of warm fresh bread to break apart and rub over *her* fancy walls till the soft crumbs rolled to the floor.

8

Ellen

I had waited nearly the whole day by the parlour window. It afforded the best view of the street. I curled up on the cushioned window seat and watched the maids from the houses opposite bring in freshly filled milk jugs from their doorsteps. I watched market carts rolling down the street and knots of children being hurried along on their morning walks. I watched countless cabs rumble past. Not one pulled up outside our house.

I had Mary bring me a tray of tea and I sat there and I waited and I waited. Doors were opened and closed, people came and went and soon there was nothing left to watch. Then, just as the day began to dim and the lamp-lighter wandered down the street, with his lighting rod balanced on his shoulder, two sleek, black horses and a dark green carriage appeared from the end of the street and pulled up outside the railings.

My heart leapt and I pressed my face to the window. The door of the carriage opened and a young man stepped out. He stood for a moment under the glow of a lamp and looked up at the house. I held my breath. I noticed his lips at first; they were full and ruddy and turned up into a half smile. His hair was dark as treacle and his eyes were hidden under a long fringe. He was wearing a black mourning suit and, with his black gloves and black cravat, he looked like a young boy in man's clothing. Part of me wanted him to see me standing there behind the lace curtains. But he did not. Instead, he looked away and nodded to the driver to fetch his bags.

I quickly pulled the lace to one side and, as he turned back to climb the steps to the front door, he flicked his hair back and glanced over at me. He had the greenest of eyes. I should have dropped the curtains, or at least have averted my gaze or turned my head. But I just stood there. My newly tightened corset made it impossible for me to breathe evenly and I could feel a hotness spreading from my cheeks down to my powdered bosom. Mary had brought me a tin of arrowroot from the larder and had insisted on dusting the white powder over my cheeks and chest. 'It's what all the young ladies use, miss,' she had reassured me. I hoped the pleasing pearly whiteness was not disappearing now under a flush of unbecoming scarlet.

Jacob Grey smiled at me slowly and I swallowed down the saliva that had gathered in my mouth as I heard Mary open the door to him.

She took him straight to Father's study. I had more than an hour to wait before dinner and I could barely contain myself. I called Mary to my bedroom and she tried a new arrangement for my hair. It was the latest fashion, she said, all curls and fancy twists. I looked at my reflection in the mirror and wondered what Jacob Grey would see. I wished my hair were light and golden and not heavy and black as coal. I wished my eyes were blue instead of dull brown, and I wished my neck were pale and graceful as a swan's. I hated my plain black mourning gown and was glad that as Isabella Grey was just an aunt, I would only have to wear it for six weeks.

'How do I look, Mary?' I asked.

'Beautiful, miss. A fine picture indeed.'

'No, truthfully,' I said. 'Do I not look too dull all in black?' She stuck more pins into the pile of hair on my head and stood back to consider.

'Truthfully, miss,' she said. 'You look a picture.'

I caught her hand and squeezed it tight, my stomach churning with excitement.

I hurried at last to the dining room. Father eyed my hair and frowned as I walked round the table. Mother was sitting in her usual place, dabbing at her top lip with a handkerchief. She did not even look at me. Jacob Grey stood immediately and pulled my chair out. I nodded my gratitude and blushed furiously as I smoothed my skirts and sat.

It was the longest of dinners. Ninny had cooked up a boiled calf's head and had inserted a bunch of wilting parsley in both of the poor creature's eye sockets. The air was damp and smelt of vegetable steam and gristle. All I wanted to do was to look at Jacob Grey, but I kept my head down and looked instead at the flap of calf's cheek and slice of pink tongue sitting on my plate.

Mary moved around the room filling glasses and plates and removing empty dishes. Cutlery chinked on china and the sounds of Father's chewing and swallowing made me wince.

'Sir?' Jacob Grey's voice burst across the table. 'Thank you again for having me to stay.'

Father kept sawing at the meat on his plate and did not reply. I willed him to answer, but the silence grew longer. I could feel my face burning and I wanted to slide under the table. How could he be this rude? Why had he not even introduced Jacob to me and Mother? As if he had read my thoughts Jacob tried again.

'Aunt Eliza. You have a lovely home. And Ellen. It's good to meet you. I never knew I had such a beautiful cousin.'

He had called me beautiful. Jacob Grey had called me beautiful. Father looked up slowly from his plate. Gravy dripped from the fork he held in front of his mouth.

'Please refrain from talking at the table, Jacob. Conversation will be reserved until after dinner, when we gather together in the drawing room.'

The clock on the mantelpiece ticked and I found myself chewing in time to it.

'Well, I shall look forward to that, sir,' said Jacob. Father looked back to his plate but I saw his hand tighten around his wine glass. After a while, I dared to glance at my cousin. His neck was flushed red and he had barely touched his food.

Dinner was eventually finished and Father ushered us into the drawing room. He busied himself with a cigar and I sat down on the couch with my sewing. Jacob walked slowly around the room, studying the paintings on the walls and the ornaments on tables and shelves. He was so handsome; I could not stop looking at him. His skin was clear, his nose was straight and his hair fell below his collar in clean, shiny waves. There was no trace of the heavily sweet macassar oil that Father was in the habit of smoothing into his own hair. I looked at Jacob's hands; they looked so strong for a boy. He had broad fingers and polished nails and small dark hairs grew on his wrists. As he passed close by me I caught his scent. He smelt of lemons, sharp and bitter, and it made my mouth water.

The drawing room was stuffy; the fire cracked and sputtered, sending its heat out in rolling blasts. Mother, forced by Father's steely stare to join us for a while, was snoring in her chair; a thin string of saliva hung from the corner of her mouth. I saw Jacob glance over at her and he caught me looking at him and crinkled his eyes. I felt as if we had shared a delightful secret.

9

Queenie

It seemed not a week went by that Mam didn't bring a strange man home with her. The sheet hung across the room was never taken down. Sometimes when it wasn't pulled across right, Queenie caught a glimpse of shabby boots or the legs of fine woollen trousers. Mam had coins in the purse around her neck now. There was money for food and coal for the fire. But Mam didn't seem to care. She didn't klatter on any more, or sing her songs or tell her stories. She was like a ghost who drifted through the days without ever really being there. She had given up on Da coming back, Queenie knew she had.

The news that Mam had taken to selling her body spread quickly through the alleys and back streets of Blackfriars. Queenie couldn't think of Mam as being a whore. She wasn't like the others. She didn't paint her face or leave the buttons of her bodice undone. She didn't spend her days at the gin-shop sitting on the laps of drunken men. She wasn't like Dirty Sal from out the back. *She* cursed like a sailor and spent her earnings on blue ruin instead of bread for her five children. Mam didn't have to go looking for customers. Mam was a beauty. Da was always telling her so. A rare flower.

Queenie took the little ones out on the streets. The grunts of those faceless men and the thought of Mam with her skirts up round her swollen belly were more than she could bear. She hoisted Albie onto her hip and held Kit's hand as they wandered through the back alleys. Tally trailed along behind, but he kept close to Queenie, tugging her skirt every now and then.

'Where we going?' he asked. 'Can we stop now? Me feet 'urt.'

'In a minute,' said Queenie. She didn't know where they were going, but she knew Tally's feet would be burning with the cold. It was Kit's turn to wear the boots.

They turned a corner into Friar Street. It led to Waterloo Station. There would be hot salted potatoes to be had from the barrows lined up to tempt hungry passengers and maybe, thought Queenie, today would be the day she spotted Da's face in the crowds.

Part way down the road Queenie saw three women stood in the doorway of a pawnshop. They were all of them wearing bonnets, the lace on the edges frayed and yellowed. One of them was smoking a pipe. As Queenie and the little ones came closer, she took it from her mouth and pointed it towards them.

'Look who we have 'ere,' she sneered. 'The hoity-toity whore's little bastards.' Queenie gripped Albie tighter and tugged Kit's hand. She turned her head.

'Tally!' she hissed. 'Keep up!'

'You tell your mam we ain't too pleased with her goings-on,' said the woman, with a smirk. 'Pinchin' our custom without so much as a thank you. You tell her to watch 'er back. That pretty little face of 'ers mightn't be so pretty for much longer.'

The woman turned back to her friends. They cackled and stared at Queenie as she walked past, her heart thumping loudly. Was Mam going to end up like that? Hard and ugly, and even more worn out than she already was? Queenie felt so tired all of a sudden. She wanted to find a warm corner to curl up in and sleep and sleep. Then she wanted to wake up far from here and not have to think of the little ones or look at Mam's face or keep hoping that Da would come home. It had been too long now. The part of Queenie that still believed he would come back was getting smaller and smaller.

Waterloo Station was busy. The smell of hot oil, coal and smoke hit the back of Queenie's throat. It tasted of freedom. One day, thought Queenie. One day I'll leave here and I'll never come back. Shouts of *Hot Green Peas! Eels! Baked Taters!* reminded her that the little ones needed warming and feeding.

'Here, mind Albie,' she said to Tally as she settled them all on some steps. 'I'll just be a minute. Then you can warm your hands.'

She counted the coins in her pocket that Mam had given her earlier and dodged through the crowds towards the shouts of *Baked Taters!* Soon she had four hot bundles wrapped in newspaper clutched to her chest. The little ones' eyes lit up when they saw her coming back.

'Me! Me! Me!' they chorused and they snatched the hot taters that Queenie held out to each of them. Albie's parcel looked huge in his tiny hands. They pulled the paper off and began to nibble at the crispy skins and to suck out the steaming flesh.

'Ow!' cried Kit. 'Burnt me tongue.'

'Careful!' scolded Queenie. 'Don't scoff it so quick. And blow it first.'

She smiled to see Albie copy his big brothers; blowing hard and loud on his tater. His eyes watered as he gulped down a big lump. Queenie unwrapped her parcel and spread the sheet of newspaper out on her lap. She cupped her hands around the tater and let its warmth seep into her hands and thighs. Her eyes roamed idly over the newspaper and she began to pick out words and sentences. Mam had taught her her letters when she was only eight and Queenie could get by reading most things. MACASSAR OIL, she read. *Preserves and beautifies the hair, and prevents it falling out or turning grey.* BROWN'S SATIN POLISH. *For ladies' and children's boots and shoes.* Then an advertisement in bold letters right at the bottom of the page:

Girl wanted to assist mistress with housework and children. Mistress superintends cooking; washing sent out. Wages £8 a year. Mrs Waters, 4, Wild Street.

Queenie read the advertisement again. Wages £8. That was a fortune. Before she could think any more of it, a lump of thick brown spittle landed on the top of her tater. Queenie looked up and saw the woman with the pipe standing next to them.

'Quick,' she whispered to her brothers. 'Time to go

home.' She ripped the advertisement from the newspaper and stuffed it in her pocket. She quickly wiped the spoilt tater on her skirt and put that in her pocket too. As she urged the little ones to hurry, shepherding them back down the road, the woman laughed and shouted, 'Ha! Enjoy your meal, ducky. And don't forget to send my regards to yer mam!'

10

Ellen

'What are you making?' Jacob asked me. He had circled the drawing room twice and was now standing beside me with his hands behind his back.

'Oh, it is nothing. Just a . . . just a repair on a collar,' I stammered.

'You have very nimble fingers. My mother was the same, you know. She could mend almost anything.'

'Could she? I am sorry. I mean, not sorry she could mend things. I mean, I am sorry she is dead. I mean . . . oh . . .' I stopped. How could I be so foolish? 'I mean, you must miss her a great deal,' I managed to say.

'Yes. I do,' said Jacob. I waited for him to say more, but he took his hands from behind his back and began to study his nails. The silence grew. I did not know whether to continue with my sewing or to think of something else to say. Father was of no help. He was standing by the fireplace swirling a drink around in a glass and staring into the flames. It was as though he had forgotten there was anyone else in the room. Just when I thought I would burst with awkwardness Jacob said, 'She deserved a much better life.' He ran his fingers through his hair. 'Yes,' he said loudly. 'She deserved a much better life. Didn't she, sir?'

Father looked up and frowned. 'I am sorry your mother is no longer with us, Jacob. But I am sure she had as good a life as any of us.'

Jacob did not reply, but returned instead to studying his nails. I looked from him to Father. 'I am sure she was a wonderful lady,' I ventured. 'I only wish I could have met her.'

Jacob looked up and opened his mouth to speak.

'Enough!' shouted Father.

Mother jumped awake in her chair. 'What, what?' she mumbled.

'Ellen, take your mother to her room now. The evening has finished.'

I looked at Father. The veins in his neck were straining against his collar and his face had turned a dangerous red. I did not understand what had happened. I wanted to find out more about Jacob's mother, my Aunt Isabella. I wanted to stay near Jacob and make him see that I was not so foolish. But he had moved to the other side of the room and Mother was flapping.

'Ellen, Ellen! Come on, girl. Get me up from here.'

I sighed, put down my sewing and went to give my arm to Mother.

'Goodnight, Father. Goodnight, Jacob,' I said. Neither of them replied. I could feel an angry silence pushing me out of the door as I led Mother away.

Later in my room, as Mary was brushing out my hair, I asked her, 'Did you ever meet Aunt Isabella?'

'I did,' she replied. 'A very kind lady she was. And beautiful with it.'

'So what happened? I do not understand why she was never spoken of. Please tell me, Mary.'

'Oh, miss, don't be asking me. I don't know all the ins and outs. There was a falling out, I told you. But it is of no matter now. Your aunt has gone, but Jacob is here. So let bygones be bygones.'

'But Father is angry with him. I know he is. Why would he be angry with Jacob if it was Aunt Isabella he argued with?'

'You ask too many questions, miss. It's late now and I need to see to your mother before I turn in. Get to your bed and stop fretting. '

'Maybe Jacob will tell me,' I said quietly. 'He must be in need of a friend. And he must be all alone in the world if he had no choice but to come here.'

Mary put my hairbrush back on the dressing table and patted my shoulder gently.

'Sleep well, miss. I'll see you in the morning.'

She closed the door behind her and I sat for moment thinking of Jacob. I imagined him standing alone at his mother's graveside; throwing a handful of soil onto her coffin. A boy suddenly grown into a man. Somehow I would let him know that I understood what being lonely felt like.

11

Queenie

Queenie took the little ones the long way home. With the promise of a sixpence worth of sugared almonds, they were happy to wander slowly behind. Queenie kept a look out for Da as they walked down Lambeth Road. Every head of dark curls drew her eye. But it was never him. Searching the crowds had become more of a habit than anything else. She wasn't sure that she really wanted to find him now.

The smells of roasted meats from the chop-house drifted out on to the street and made her mouth water. She watched in envy as smart suited gentlemen greeted each other at the doorway then went inside to take their fill of all that was on offer. The little ones pressed their noses to the window of the chemist shop. Its display of coloured bottles, reds, greens, blues and yellows, glittered like polished jewels. They stood and gawped for so long that the chemist himself came out and shooed them away with a broom.

Queenie's favourite window was the draper's. She stared longingly into it at the rolls of glossy satin, the silks, ribbons, muslins and froths of lace. Queenie chose the colour silk she would have; green to match her eyes, with a trim of creamy lace and layers of muslin petticoats. She wished she could go inside. But instead she imagined the hushed air of the shop and the softness she would feel as she ran her hands over the rolls of cloth. Then Kit began to whine and she turned to see the little ones looking up at her, their snotty faces wizened by the cold. 'Sugared almonds then,' she sighed.

Mam wasn't home when they got back. The room smelt of damp coal and mouse droppings. Queenie lit a candle by the stove and sorted through the coal for some dry nuggets. She soon had a weak flame burning and the little ones settled themselves close to it. Queenie listened out for Mam, hoping madly that she'd come home alone.

'Tell us a story,' asked Tally as he rested his head on Queenie's knee. 'Go on . . . tell us one of your stories.'

'I ain't in the mood,' said Queenie.

'Why not?' asked Tally.

'I just ain't, all right?'

'Mam won't tell us any no more,' whispered Tally. 'Don't see why you can't instead.'

'Cause maybe I've run out of stories too!' shouted Queenie. 'Besides, I got other things on me mind, right?'

Tally was silent. Queenie felt a twinge of guilt. None of it was his fault, she thought. But then it wasn't her fault either. She hadn't asked for this life, she didn't want this life. The baby was well out of it. She was glad it had died. It wouldn't have to grow up with hunger and cold and dirt being the only things to wake up to in the mornings. It could just sleep forever.

The door banged open suddenly and Queenie turned round expecting to see Mam. But it wasn't Mam. It was a man in a dark overcoat with glaring eyes and a whiskery chin. He was carrying a cane and swaying slightly where he stood in the doorway.

'So,' he said, looking around with a sneer. 'Here's the place for a spot of pleasure, I believe.'

'Who are you?' asked Queenie, moving closer to the little ones. 'What do you want?'

'I don't believe that is the way things are done,' said the man as he removed his gloves. 'Discretion is the word, is it not? Now do you have another room for us to go to? I draw the line at an audience.' He nodded towards Tally, Kit and Albie.

Queenie felt a knot of fear rise in her throat. 'I don't know who you are,' she said. 'And I don't know what you want. But I think you've come to the wrong place.'

'The wrong place?' said the man, raising an eyebrow. 'I don't think so. A green-eyed, dark-haired beauty? A gem amongst all the squalor? I am in the right place, I assure you. Although you are somewhat younger than I was led to believe. Now let's not waste any more of my time, girl.' He pulled a purse from his pocket and emptied two coins into his hand.

'No!' shouted Queenie in a panic. 'You've got it wrong. I ain't that sort of girl. Please, sir. Please go!'

'Ooh, a feisty one, are you? Well, any way you like it, but I will have what I came for.' He threw the coins on the floor then stepped towards Queenie and grabbed her by the arms.

'No!' she screamed. 'Get off me! Tally, get help!'

They stumbled backwards into the hanging sheet and it was pulled to the floor. The man laughed and threw Queenie on Mam's bed. He leaned over and pushed his face into hers. She could smell beer, tobacco and the thick, sweet scent of his hair oil. Queenie turned her head to one side in time to see Tally scamper from the room, his eyes wide with fright. The man held her arms down on the bed and pressed his mouth to her neck.

'Get off me!' yelled Queenie as she twisted from side to side. The man started to breathe heavily and he let go of one of her arms and began to push her skirt up and dig his fingers into her thighs. Queenie battered at him with her free hand and pulled at his hair. But he didn't stop. He began to fumble with his trousers, grunting with the effort. As his grip loosened, Queenie brought her head up and bit hard on his ear. The man fell backwards off the bed and let out a roar of pain.

'You little bitch!' he yelled.

Queenie scrambled to her feet. She could taste blood in her mouth and her legs were shaking. She needed to get out quick. She needed to get away. But Kit and Albie were standing motionless on the other side of the room. Before she could move, the door opened again and Mam walked in.

'Queenie? What's going on? Tally said to come quick. You haven't been upsetting this gentleman, have you?'

'Wha . . . what?' stammered Queenie. 'Upsetting him? Mam! He tried to force himself on me. He went for me, Mam! He went for me.'

A flicker of some sort passed across Mam's face. Then she blinked and said, 'I'm sure that's not true, Queenie.' She pushed past Queenie and went over to the man. 'There must have been some mistake. I'm so sorry, sir,' she said.

The man had now got up from the floor and was holding a handkerchief to his ear, muttering *bitch*, *bitch* over and over to himself.

'Can I help?' asked Mam. 'Get you another cloth maybe?' The man looked at her as though she was mad.

'Help?' he said. 'Help? You,' he said to Mam, 'and,' he pointed at Queenie, 'that filthy little cat, can go straight to hell!' He stumbled out the door.

Queenie was shaking, her breath coming in short angry sobs. Tally had come back in and was standing behind Mam looking warily around the room.

'Mam?' Queenie whispered. 'How . . . how could you be like that with him? He . . . he attacked me!'

Mam bent to pick up the coins from the floor. 'He just thought you were me,' she said. 'That's all. No harm done.'

'No harm? But . . . but, if you hadn't come back?'

'Well, I did. I'm sorry, Queenie, but I can't afford to upset customers. Word gets round fast, you know.'

'But what about me?' said Queenie, her voice wavering. 'What about all of *us*?'

'All of you?' shouted Mam. 'All of you! And this one on the way?' She jabbed her belly with a finger. 'Who do think I'm doing this for? Do you think I want any of this? Do you think I have a choice?'

'There must be another way,' said Queenie, taking a deep breath.

'Well, there isn't,' said Mam, her face closing up. 'It's this or the workhouse. You choose.'

'But there's people out there saying nasty things about you!' said Queenie.

Mam ignored her. 'I said, it's this or the workhouse. You choose.'

Queenie lay awake all night. The close warmth of Tally, Kit and Albie gave her no comfort. Da wasn't coming back and Mam was a stranger. She shivered, thinking of the man and how the weight of him on top of her had made her lose her breath; and how he had made her feel so small and useless and dirty. She thought of the woman with the pipe and her nasty words. And she thought of Mam not caring, and her coldness. She felt in her pocket for the torn advertisement and listened to the steady breathing of the little ones.

As the pale light of morning edged into the room, Queenie heard the door slowly creak open. She stiffened. Was it him again? The man from earlier? She looked towards the sound and saw the bulk of a male body filling the doorway. A shout rose up from her chest, but before it reached her throat, the body stepped into the room and Queenie saw the unmistakeable dark curls on Da's head.

'Da!' she whispered loudly, relief relaxing her tightened muscles.

'Sshh!' he said, grinning at her like some dirty urchin. With one finger waving wildly in front of his mouth, he staggered over to the bed and fell on to it. Mam let out a startled cry which quickly turned to a soft moan. Queenie listened to their muffled whispers, the wet noise of their kisses and their breathing becoming faster and faster.

She couldn't bear it. Wasn't Mam even angry with him? Couldn't Da smell the other men on Mam? Queenie pushed her fists into her ears. Was that it then? Everything back to how it always was. Until the next time Da buggered off? Would her and Mam take it in turns to do the whoring then? Mam had said there was no choice. Maybe there wasn't for her; saddled with Da and the little ones. But Mam is Mam, thought Queenie. And I ain't her.

The little ones hadn't stirred and Queenie lay still too, shaping the thought in her head that was growing bigger and bigger. She took her fists from her ears. All was quiet as she fingered the torn advertisement again.

When the sound of Da's breathing turned to heavy snores, Queenie rose quietly from the pile of straw and kissed first Kit, then Albie gently on the cheek. She looked at Tally and his serious little face, his constant frown relaxed in sleep. She whispered so as not to wake him, 'You'll be all right without me, won't you? You're a big lad now.' She bent to kiss him too. Then with a last fleeting look at the heap of Mam and Da on the bed, Queenie crept out of the door.

12

Ellen

Mary came to me the following morning fizzing with excitement. 'Seems the young man will be with us for a while then, miss,' she said.

'What do you mean, Mary?'

'They're saying downstairs that he's to be your father's apprentice!'

'Father's apprentice?' I breathed.

Mary nodded. 'I believe so. It'll do this house good to have another young person in it. Do you good too, to have the company.'

'Oh, Mary!' I stood and put my arms around her and hugged her tightly. I hoped that what she said was true. I hoped Jacob would stay long enough for us to get to know one another. For us to become friends, even.

Although Father made no official announcement, every day after that, Jacob left the breakfast table when Father did and rode with him in his carriage to the University College Hospital. After every silent dinner Father had Jacob in the drawing room and they talked about his studies and of things that made no sense to me. They barely noticed me sitting in the corner with my sewing. I did not even have

Mother for company. She had taken to having her meals sent to her room; declaring herself too exhausted to come downstairs. It was not how I had wanted it to be.

Every day my head was filled with imagined walks around the garden with Jacob; imagined confidences and conversations. But all my imagined words were stuck in my throat with nowhere to go. I could only look at him from across the table or from across the room.

'You must eat more, miss,' Mary said to me. 'Your gowns are getting loose.'

'But I have no appetite. I have no interest in eating.' I sighed. 'I have no interest in anything, Mary. I cannot even read my books. What is wrong with me?'

Mary gave me a gentle smile. 'You are just unsettled, miss . . . with the young man being in the house and all. And maybe you are letting your notions run away with you?'

I blushed and lowered my head. 'What notions? I have barely even talked to Jacob. And besides,' I protested, 'he is my cousin!'

Mary laughed. 'That is of no matter, as you well know!' she said. 'Our own Queen Victoria married her cousin!' She winked at me. 'He's on your mind too much, isn't he, miss? That's exactly what is vexing you.'

She was right; she knew me too well. 'Oh, Mary, what am I to do? I cannot think of anything else but him. I only want to be his friend. But there is never the opportunity to talk. I do not think he even notices me.'

'Nonsense, miss. Of course he notices you. I have seen the way he glances over at you when you're not looking. He notices you. Mark my words.'

'Truly? Does he, Mary?'

'He does, miss, I assure you.'

'But how we will ever get the chance to get to know each other?'

'Just you wait, miss. Be patient and your time will come. In the meantime try and eat a little more. A true lady should never come to resemble a bag of bones, believe you me.'

Mary's words came true the very next day. Jacob did not appear at breakfast. Father left for the hospital by himself and Mary whispered to me that Jacob had asked for tea to be brought to him in the library. I looked at her in surprise. She winked at me and said, 'I can't see there'll be any harm in me bringing two cups. Can you, miss?'

Before I could answer, Mary picked up a tray of unused dishes and bustled out of the dining room. I sat at the empty breakfast table, thinking of Jacob just a few rooms away. A moment later I found myself walking along the hallway towards the library, my heart thumping loudly beneath my morning gown.

The library door was closed. I reached out for the handle, but could not bring myself to turn it. Suddenly all the imagined conversations disappeared from my head. He was in there, behind the door, all on his own. I could just walk in right now. I knew I should not. It was against all that was proper. But what harm could come of it? I had no idea what I would say. What if he *wanted* to be on his own? What if I was an annoyance to him? I swallowed hard. I would just go in, I decided, and pretend I had lost a book. If he seemed in need of company I would stay. If not, I would quickly leave.

I opened the door and walked in. Jacob was leaning back against a bookcase with his arms folded looking straight at me. 'Good morning, Ellen,' he said. 'I knew you'd come.'

'How . . . how . . . how did you? I am . . . I am just looking for my book,' I said hurriedly. 'I thought I might have left it in here.'

Jacob spread his arms wide. 'Do you see it anywhere?'

'I . . . I do not know,' I said. I began to search the bookshelves. I pulled out books and examined the covers. I dropped a couple on the floor and hastily put them back in place. I picked up a book left on a table and began to flick through the pages. It was a medical dictionary, I realised, and I was holding it upside down.

'Have you found it yet?' asked Jacob. He was smiling.

'No . . . no. Not yet,' I said. I was hot, and flustered. Jacob began to laugh softly. He was teasing me and I felt like a stupid child. I wished I had never started my pretence. Mary came in with a tray of tea and set it down on the table by the window.

'Thank you, Mary,' said Jacob cheerily. 'Are you thirsty?' he asked me. 'I see Mary has brought two cups.'

It was happening. Jacob was in front of me. We were on our own and he wanted me to stay. My hands were damp and part of me wanted to run from the room. But I knew I would not. I knew this was all I truly wanted. We sat by the window looking out on the garden. My hands shook slightly as I poured the tea.

55

'So,' said Jacob. 'What is it you are reading at the moment? What is this book you have lost?'

I blushed. He knew there was no book, but how could I admit to it? And how could I tell him I had not been able to read a word since his arrival? 'Oh, it is nothing,' I said. 'You would find it tedious if I told you. So . . .' I said quickly. 'Why have you not gone with Father today to the hospital?'

He looked at me seriously. 'You think it is wrong of me to want to spend some time getting to know my cousin?'

'Wr . . . wrong?' I stammered. Had he really stayed at home just to see me? 'No . . . no, I do not think it is wrong. Although in truth we should be chaperoned,' I added shyly.

Jacob laughed.

'I do wonder at Father allowing you a day away from the hospital, though,' I continued. 'He is very strict in his ways.'

Jacob's eyes flashed with mischief. 'Your father is only too happy to let me do as I please. I assure you.'

'That does not sound like Father at all,' I said, surprised. 'He must be impressed with your progress. How are your studies?'

I did not like to think of Jacob's hands touching those dead bodies. It did not suit him somehow. He was too alive to be spending his days in that hideous yellow room. He did not answer straight away. He was looking at me closely and his gaze made me turn away.

'I am not here to talk about my studies, Ellen.' He reached out his hand and gently turned my face back towards him. 'You are so beautiful,' he whispered.

'Oh! I . . . I . . .' I was so surprised and shocked by his touch that I stood in a rush and knocked a teacup to the floor. 'I . . . I am so sorry,' I whispered.

Jacob smiled and bent to pick up the cup. 'Sit down, Ellen,' he said. 'Where are you going?'

A strange sensation flittered up and down my spine and my face prickled with heat. I could still feel the trace of Jacob's fingers on the skin of my cheek. It felt unbearably good.

'I . . . I just need to clean this before it stains,' I said, indicating the splashes of tea on the folds of my skirts. 'I . . . I . . . I just need to see to this.'

I turned and began to walk from the room. I had to leave. My heart was pounding. Why was I acting like such a fool?

'Ellen?' said Jacob.

'Yes?' I replied, and dared myself to turn round.

'I think we are going to be good friends. You and I.' He stared at me and touched his fingers to his lips.

I hesitated for a moment. I desperately wanted to stay, but I had to regain my composure. I did not want him to think me a complete idiot.

'I hope we will be,' I replied. Then I left the room and took in a deep breath as I closed the door behind me.

13

Queenie

Queenie hurried towards Waterloo Bridge, wrapping her shawl tight around her. The air was cold and even at that early hour the streets were busy with costergirls carrying baskets and barrowmen pulling carts heaped with rags, onions, turnips and all manner of bric-a-brac. As the traffic thickened, she saw the huge grey arches of the bridge come into view. She dodged carriages and horses snorting clouds from their nostrils as they skidded on the iced roads.

She had crossed the bridge once before. A long time ago, on a hot summer's day when she was small and it was only her and Mam and Da. It was Mam who had taken her, holding her hand tightly all the way. Queenie couldn't remember the reason why they'd gone. But she had never forgotten the day. It was one of the only times she'd ever had Mam to herself.

The streets had been wider over the other side; the houses were big and white, with spaces between them. There were no children playing out and the buildings all seemed half asleep.

Mam had stood on the road, outside a house with a brass knocker in the shape of a horse's head. She stood there for a long time, hushing Queenie every time she tugged her hand. After a while, the front door opened and Mam pulled Queenie to one side. They both watched as a woman in a stiff grey gown came down the steps with a girl following behind. The girl was wearing a white dress patterned with rosebuds and had a yellow sash tied around her waist. Her dark hair was held back with a long yellow ribbon and Queenie thought it was the prettiest thing she had ever seen. The woman in grey had hurried past, not even glancing at Queenie and Mam.

'Quick, child!' the woman ordered, and Queenie watched the girl half run to keep up with her.

Mam told Queenie to stay put and had gone after the woman and girl. She'd stopped the woman, and although Queenie could hear the rise and fall of Mam's voice she couldn't make out the words. Mam bent down and said something to the girl, and then the woman in grey grabbed the girl's hand and pulled her along, away from Mam. Before she turned the corner, the girl looked around and smiled. Her face was pink and clean and the white of her dress glowed bright in the sun. Queenie had looked down at her own grubby petticoats and the holes in her boots and at that moment decided she wanted more than anything in the world to have a clean white dress and live in a grand house and be just like that girl.

'Who were they, Mam?' Queenie asked. 'Do we know them?'

'Don't be daft, girl,' Mam said in a tight voice. 'They're not our sort.'

'But you looked like you knew 'em.'

'No,' said Mam. 'It was my mistake. Now hush.'

Mam hadn't said much else on the way home; she just seemed more tired than usual and not all there. She had bought Queenie an orange and the sweet juice had washed the hot dust from Queenie's throat. Mam had never taken her across the river again, but Queenie had always remembered the girl in the white dress and the way she had taken a piece of Mam away.

Queenie reached the other side of the bridge and looked carefully at the torn piece of newspaper clutched tightly in her hand. A shopkeeper arranging his wares on a wooden trestle table looked up at her and smiled.

'Beg your pardon, mister, which way to Wild Street?'

'Wild Street? You'd be best carrying straight on for a while, young miss, up the Strand till you get to Drury Lane. Past the Nag's Head and the theatre. Look out for Wilkins Dairy. If I remember rightly, s'on the corner of Wild Street.'

'Ta very much, mister,' said Queenie.

'Anything to assist a pretty young lady,' said the shop-keeper with a wink.

Queenie looked at his eager face and stained overcoat and her head filled with a hot anger. 'Go hang yerself, you dirty dog!' she shouted over her shoulder as she walked off with her head held high.

14

Ellen

'What is it, miss? What has happened?' cried Mary as I ran into my bedroom and threw myself on the bed. 'Are you ill? Let me see your face. Let me see.' She pulled at my shoulder and I turned over and lay on my back. 'Oh, miss. You are not well.' She felt my forehead. 'You are so flushed. How do you feel?'

I burst into laughter. 'I feel wonderful, Mary. I have never felt so happy!' I thought of Jacob's eyes looking at me and the feel of his hand on my face. I could still smell his warm lemon scent. I jumped from the bed and ran over to the mirror. I hardly recognised the face that looked back at me. Tendrils of hair had escaped from their fastenings and were curled around my face. My eyes were wide and bright and my cheeks were indeed flushed a delicate pink. I *am* beautiful, I thought. I put my hand to my face where Jacob had touched me.

Everything around me seemed changed. There was colour where there did not used to be. Mary's apron was a startling white, the blue of the walls glowed bright, and the hangings on my bed shone rich reds and yellows. Even the silver of my brush on the dressing table sparkled.

Mary was watching me with a bemused look on her face. 'So, tea with Jacob went well?'

I smiled at her. I wanted to tell her how Jacob had looked at me. How he had held my face in his hand. The moment had been so beautiful it felt fragile. I decided to keep it to myself for now; to keep it safely wrapped up, like a precious gift.

'Yes, Mary. It went well.' I sighed and pulled at the loose strands of my hair. 'You can leave that for now.' I nodded towards the pile of linen that Mary was sorting through and turned back to my reflection in the mirror. 'But come back later and fix my hair before dinner.'

'As you please, miss,' she said, walking towards the door. 'If you're sure you are feeling well?'

'Quite well, thank you,' I replied. 'Oh, Mary, it is so good to have him here, is it not?'

Mary's reply was lost as she closed my bedroom door behind her.

One of Father's colleagues joined us for dinner that evening. He was a fair-haired young man with pleasant eyes who seemed uncomfortable in his stiff suit and starched collar. Usually I would have studied him with interest, being so unused to outside company. But apart from his annoying habit of pulling at the end of his nose at frequent intervals, he left no impression on me.

Jacob was concentrating on his meal and barely looked up from his plate. I caught his eye only once, when he lifted his head to nod thanks to Mary for refilling his glass. The expected smile in my direction never came and heavy disappointment took away the little appetite I had. He is just being discreet, I told myself. A real gentleman would never allude to our earlier intimacy. I tried to eat a little potato, but it seemed to fill my whole mouth and I had to force it down with a sip of wine.

I hoped that the visitor would occupy Father in the drawing room and Jacob would be left free to sit by me and maybe pass me pins as I sewed. But he stayed close to Father and our guest, even though he did not join in their conversation. He seemed intent on keeping his back to me and I began to wonder if I'd imagined our exchange in the library. There was no need for him to be this cold. I pricked my finger on my needle and although the pain was very slight, it brought tears to my eyes which felt hot and foolish.

It seemed an eternity before Mary came in to take Mother to bed. Blood had stained the small embroidery I was working on, but I did not care. I wanted to leave the room too, as quickly as I could, and be on my own in my bed. I put down my sewing and bade the men goodnight. Although our guest broke off from conversation to wish me a good evening, Father merely grunted and Jacob nodded his head.

I told Mary I could put myself to bed once she had unlaced me and hung up my gown. She did not protest, probably being only too glad for an early night. The quietness of my room was all that I wanted, and as I heard Mary's footsteps disappear down the corridor, I let myself feel what had been filling my insides all evening.

I sat on the edge of my bed and thumped my pillows hard. How dare he make me feel like this? To ignore me so rudely? No harm would have come from him showing some politeness. I was not going to cry. I would show him that it did not matter to me in the least. He was only a poor orphan, after all. I deserved much better, didn't I?

I unpinned my hair and sat at my dressing table brushing through the tangles with quick, hard strokes. I would not go down to breakfast in the morning, I decided. I would feign some complaint and stay in my room.

A small tap at my door made me pause in my brushing. Mary checking on me, no doubt. I fancied I could do with her company now and she may as well finish my hair while she was here. My arm was beginning to ache. 'Come in!' I called. The door did not open. 'Mary. Come in!' I called again. Still she did not open the door. What was she doing? I put my brush down on the dressing table and, wrapping my shawl around me, I went to open the door myself.

There was no one outside. The corridor was empty. Foolish woman, I thought. She must be getting deaf in her old age and assumed I was asleep. As I went to close the door I saw a fold of paper lying on the floor just inside the threshold. I picked it up, closed the door and went over to the candle by my bed to see what it was. My fingers fumbled as I unfolded the paper.

Ellen

I will be back early from the hospital tomorrow. I will be in the garden at around three o'clock if you would care to take a stroll.

Yours,

Jacob

I laughed out loud and hugged the note to me. How could I have doubted him? I had been childish and impatient. Now I just wanted the hours to pass, for the night to disappear in a blink and for me to be walking through the garden to meet Jacob. I chided myself for my continued impatience, and felt a smile stretch across my face as I slipped the note under my pillow and climbed into bed to wait for sleep to come.

15

Queenie

Wild Street was quiet. Its grubby four-storeyed houses seemed to Queenie to be the grandest of places. They stood tall and proud and stared down their noses at the rest of the world. She looked again at the name on the piece of newspaper. *Mrs Waters,* she whispered to herself, *I've come about the position, ma'am.* She smoothed down her hair and straightened her shawl and hoped that no one would notice how Mam's old shoes slopped about on her feet.

Number 4 was the second house on the left. Its windows were streaked with dirt and the tiny front garden was a tangle of overgrown weeds. Queenie took a deep breath, climbed the ten steps up to the door and knocked hard.

Footsteps echoed inside the house and Queenie heard locks being unbolted. Then a large woman with untidy orange curls opened the door and peered out.

'Erm, sorry to disturb you, ma'am. Mrs Waters I'm after. Is she home?'

'What is it you want her for?'

'She needs a girl to help her with the housework and the children. Here, look, I saw it in the newspaper.' Queenie held the torn paper advertisement out to the woman.

'Yes, yes,' said the woman impatiently. 'Well, *I* am Mrs

Waters, but I'm afraid you don't look like the sort of girl I'm after.' She went to close the door and Queenie's heart sank. She didn't want to find somewhere to sleep on the streets or worse, walk back home.

'But please, ma'am,' she said quickly. 'Can't you give me a chance? I ain't scared of hard work and there's enough little 'uns at home for me to have learned what to do with 'em. I'd be a good worker, ma'am, if you'd just let me show you.'

Mrs Waters paused and looked Queenie up and down. 'You've had plenty of dealings with children, you say?'

'Yes, ma'am.'

'And babies?'

'Oh yes, ma'am. Plenty. Me Mam is always having new little 'uns.'

'So why aren't you at home helping her?'

'No more room for me, ma'am. And besides we had a falling out and I'm making my own way in the world now.' Queenie stood tall and straight.

'Well . . . you'd have to live in anyway, you know. Tend to the babies in the night if need be. And keep the house in order and fetch the children's milk.'

'Yes ma'am, course ma'am. I could do all that.'

'And does your mother know you're here?'

'Oh no, ma'am. Not yet she don't.'

'Well . . . maybe I'll give you a go, then. Just a day or two, mind. See how you get on. Have you brought your things with you?'

'Don't have any things, ma'am. Only what I have on. But I'll keep myself clean I will.'

'Well, you'd better come in, then.' Mrs Waters looked up and down the street. 'And tell me your name, girl.'

'Yes, sorry, ma'am. It's Queenie, ma'am. I'm fourteen, and I'm ever so grateful to you.'

Queenie hardly dared to say anything else in case she was dreaming. And if she was dreaming she didn't want to wake up. A maid! She was going to be a maid in a grand house. And be trusted to look after the mistress's children too. She wondered if she would have a uniform and a cap, or some new shoes at least.

Mrs Waters shut the front door and bolted it. 'Come on then, girl, you may as well start as you mean to go on.'

Queenie looked around as she followed Mrs Waters' bustling back. The hallway was bigger than their whole room at home, with a fancy dark-wood staircase that curled up and round and disappeared from view. There were faded paintings of stern-looking gentlemen on the walls and the floor was tiled with small squares of red, green and yellow which Mrs Waters' shoes clacked on as she hurried ahead. She led Queenie through a door at the end and down a dark stairwell.

'This is the back kitchen,' she said, 'where you'll be doing most of your work. You'll sleep here too. There's a mattress in the scullery.'

Another woman, shorter and scrawnier than Mrs Waters but with the same orange hair scraped back in a bun, was standing mixing something in a jug at the kitchen table.

'Sarah, this is Queenie. Answered our advertisement to help out with the babies. Queenie, this is Mrs Ellis. My sister. You'll be taking your orders from her too.'

Queenie nodded, but couldn't reply. The sight that met her eyes was far too astonishing. Lying on a worn sofa at the back of the kitchen was an untidy row of babies. All squashed close together with barely a stitch on any of them. Eight? Nine? Ten? Queenie didn't have time to count properly before she saw the two wooden crates on the floor. They had babies inside too. A couple in each at least.

'These are all *your* children?' she asked before she could stop herself.

'Yes, in a manner of speaking,' said Mrs Waters. 'But it is not your place to ask questions. You understand?'

'Yes,' replied Queenie, feeling more and more uncomfortable.

'Good. Then we'll say no more. You work hard, we pay your wages and then . . . we shall all get along just fine, won't we? Now . . . you can help Mrs Ellis with the morning feeds.'

'Yes ma'am,' said Queenie. She suddenly realised why the room was making her feel so uneasy. Not one of the babies was making a sound. Not a whimper or a whine of hunger. They were all lying as still as still could be, their eyes open and staring. Queenie knew enough about babies to know that was just not right.

16

Ellen

It was a bitter cold afternoon. Not a day to be leaving the comforts of the parlour fire. But warm anticipation had been flowing through me since I'd woken that morning and I barely felt the need for the winter cloak and bonnet that Mary pressed upon me.

'Don't stay out too long, miss,' she warned me. 'I don't want you getting the chills. And mind your father does not hear of this. You know he would not approve of you and Jacob meeting alone.'

'Do not fuss, Mary,' I told her. 'I will be discreet. And please hurry with my bonnet!'

She finished tying the ribbons under my chin and I hurried out to the garden. The air outside stung my cheeks with its delicious coldness. As I walked down the steps of the terrace on to the path that led away from the house, I tried to calm myself and slow my pace.

The garden was quite bare except for a smattering of evergreen shrubs planted at intervals along the borders, but as I walked further along, I noticed the bright white of daphne flowers blinking at me and golden patches of winter aconite nestled underneath the trees. Where was Jacob, though? The garden was not so large for me to have to hunt him out.

'Ellen!' Jacob's voice sounded from behind me and I turned to see him hurrying along the path towards me. I felt my cheeks grow hot, despite the cold.

'Ellen!' he said, as he came up beside me. 'I hope I haven't kept you waiting for too long?'

'No . . . no,' I assured him. 'I have only been out here for a moment.'

'Good,' he said. Then he took my hand and hooked it in the crook of his arm as if it was the most natural thing in the world.

We walked in silence for a while, around the walled flower garden and back up the pathway to face the house. Jacob stopped and I turned to look at him, expecting him to say something. But he was staring at the house. I took the opportunity to study his profile; the way his skin darkened along his jaw line and the slight dimple in his cheek.

'You are very fortunate,' he said, still looking at the house. 'To live in such a place. To have such a life.'

His words took me by surprise. 'Yes, I suppose I am,' I said. I did not want to sound ungrateful and I could not tell him how dull and empty my life usually was. 'I have never really thought about it before.'

'Of course you haven't. My beautiful cousin. Why would you have had to?' He was looking at me now and smiling. I felt encouraged to continue the conversation.

'Did you not live in a house like this one? Before, I mean? Before your mother passed away?'

'Ha! Oh, Ellen,' he said. 'Your father really didn't tell you anything, did he?'

'No,' I said quietly. 'I did not even know he had a sister.

71

Or that I had a cousin. All I know,' I ventured, 'is what Mary has told me since.'

'And what is that?' asked Jacob.

'That my father and your mother had a falling out.'

Jacob began walking again and I gripped the crook of his elbow to keep pace with him. 'My mother was a good woman, Ellen,' he said. She was a friend of the poor, you know. Not long after I was born we were forced to move from London to a small village. Father was ill and Mother nursed him until he died. Then she carried on; nursing the sick, visiting the poor and cheering up the old and infirm. Not much of a life, was it? She should have had so much more. She *could* have had so much more.' He paused. 'So, no, Ellen. I never did live in a house like this one.'

He suddenly turned to me and took hold of both my hands. 'Anyway,' he said. 'Enough of boring old me. It's freezing out here! What do you say we go inside, get Mary to bring us hot drinks and I'll challenge you to a game of Old Maid!' He started to run, pulling me along with him, and by the time we were back inside we were both out of breath and laughing.

The following month was the most heavenly month of my whole life. Jacob chose not to go to the hospital every day, and sought me out time and time again when Father was out of the house. He strolled with me in the garden and we talked of books and clouds and examined each other's knowledge of shrubs and flowers. Jacob invariably knew more than me and I was flattered that someone so clever should take such notice of me. He read me passages from his favourite books and I thrilled to hear of Jules Verne's *A Journey to the Centre of the Earth* and of Dr Frankenstein and his hideous monster. I did not tell Jacob that Dr Frankenstein's laboratory reminded me of Father's dissecting room. I concentrated instead on the sound of Jacob's voice and the way it changed when he spoke the words of different characters.

I loved to watch his face as he talked; the way his lips moved as he formed words, the glimpse of his tongue as he moistened his lips between sentences and the way his eyebrows drew close together during a particularly harrowing or exciting passage. Most of all I loved it when he smiled or laughed. The sorrow that lurked behind his eyes disappeared at those times. He became carefree, and I wanted to always make him feel like that.

He never talked of his mother and I did not take it upon myself to ask. One day, though, a silence fell between us and Jacob leaned towards me and looked directly into my eyes.

'Mother would have approved of you,' he said.

I looked back at him; at the flecks of grey in the green of his eyes. A strange longing filled my insides and I began to tremble. He was so close I felt the warmth of his breath on my face. I knew I should pull away, but I could not move. Instead I closed my eyes. At that moment he put his lips on mine and kissed me softly. I could not help but sigh. I felt as helpless and weak as a baby bird, and it was a while before I could bring myself to open my eyes again. When I dared to look at him, Jacob was smiling foolishly and I felt like a shy child. But I knew then, with a certainty, that we were now sealed together forever.

That night as Mary was brushing out my hair I stopped her hand and said, 'Mary, have you ever been in love?'

'Once or twice.' She winked. 'A long time ago, mind.'

'So you know what it feels like, then?'

'Can't say as I do. It was so long ago.'

'It can't have been proper love, then, Mary. You would never have forgotten if you had ever felt like this.'

'You go careful, miss.' Mary looked worried. 'Don't fall too hard too soon. After all, we don't know the boy that well yet, do we?'

'Oh, Mary! What is there to know? He has lost his mother, he is all alone in the world and he has come here to us, his only family.'

'I am just saying, miss. Take care. Take care of your feelings.'

'Why are you saying this, Mary? I thought you would be glad for me.'

'I . . . I am glad for you, miss. But . . .'

'But what, Mary? What is it?'

'Well, I didn't like to say anything, miss, but . . . I just have a feeling that something isn't quite right. And Ninny has been overhearing things.'

'Ninny? What things has she been hearing?'

'Well, raised voices, mostly, coming from your father's study. Your father and Jacob arguing.'

'And what were they arguing about?'

'Oh, you know Ninny. She couldn't quite make it out.'

'I am sure it is nothing, Mary.' I laughed. 'I expect Jacob

dared to question one of Father's opinions, that is all!' I pictured Jacob's tender smile and his fearless green eyes. 'He is not afraid you know, Mary. He is not afraid of Father one bit.'

'I know,' she said as she turned to leave. 'That's what worries me.'

I had thought that only Mary knew of my meetings with Jacob, but one day Father called me to his study and told me that on no account was I to spend time in Jacob's company on my own. It would be entirely improper for me to behave in such a manner he said, and it was his duty as my father to prevent my reputation from being sullied. I would be committing the gravest of errors if I were to disobey him.

But for all his harsh words and despite the fear that curdled in my stomach, I could not stop myself.

The days slipped by, one drifting into the next. Days that were filled with Jacob. Thoughts of Jacob, dreams of Jacob and delicious stolen moments spent together. Poor Mary was torn in two. She did not want to disobey Father's orders, but she could see that I would not be told.

'Please be careful, miss,' she pleaded. 'You know your father has eyes everywhere.'

Father was silent. More silent than usual. He spent the evenings in the drawing room reading his paper while Jacob and I were forced to break the quiet with snippets of polite conversation. Jacob still went most days with Father to the hospital, but on some days he returned early on his own and on other days he did not go at all. It was those times I lived for.

Spring had come early and the walled flower garden was alive with colour: yellow buttercups, pink campions, lilac violas and white clouds of cow parsley. It was here we met, on the bench behind the carved stone archway, hidden from view. The household had come out of mourning for Aunt Isabella and I was able to wear my prettiest gowns again. On the day I wore my pale yellow silk, Jacob picked me a posy of daisies and sprinkled them in my hair. He looked at me thoughtfully. 'My mother was very beautiful too, you know. And kind.'

I nodded and waited, hoping he would tell me more.

'She was too kind for her own good,' he said, picking the petals off a buttercup one by one. 'Too kind and too stubborn in her ways. She and your father fell out when I was just a baby.' He crushed the remains of the buttercup in the palm of his hand.

I nodded again, encouraging him to continue.

'She wanted nothing more to do with him. And he wanted nothing more to do with her. I could never under-stand it.' He stood and began to kick softly at the borders of cow parsley. The tiny white flowers trembled on their stems, some falling to the ground.

'What happened?' I ventured. He didn't seem to hear me.

'When my father died,' he continued, 'she could have asked your father for help. For money. He has all this, after all.' Jacob spread his arms wide. 'But she didn't. She had too much pride.' He pressed down on the tiny white flowers with his foot, crushing them to powder. 'We were so poor.' He looked at me and his face had changed. It was hard and angry. 'And here you are,' he said, 'with all this! All of this that could have been shared.'

'I . . . I am sorry, Jacob.' I didn't know what to say. I suddenly felt awkward and wished Mary would come looking for me.

Then Jacob sat back down. He was smiling again. 'Ah, Ellen!' he sighed. 'It is so good to breathe in this air and to see things alive and growing. You cannot know what it is like in that hospital. Darkness and death and rot.'

I was about to tell him that I did know, that I still had nightmares about that awful day Father had taken me there, but he turned suddenly and grabbed my shoulders, fingers digging hard into my skin. Tears sprang instantly to my eyes.

'It is not the life for me, Ellen. But I *will* have the life I deserve!' He let go of me and got to his feet.

'Jacob?' I said quietly. 'Jacob?' But he was walking away, back to the house. 'Jacob!' I called after him. He did not turn round.

As he disappeared from view I saw my tears had spilt on to my skirts and darkened the silk.

17

Queenie

Queenie had been at Wild Street for nearly two months and already life with Mam and Da and the little ones seemed an age away. She hardly ever thought of them all. Only sometimes the little ones came to mind; mostly in the quiet of the evening when Mrs Waters had gone out, the babies had been dosed and Mrs Ellis had at last taken herself off to her room. Mrs Ellis was always about. Telling Queenie to sweep the brick floors of the kitchen, rake out the ashes and fetch in coal and wood from the yard. And always to mind the babies.

There were a couple of other ladies in the house too, timid things with growing bellies under their loosened gowns. They stayed in their rooms all day at the top of the house and Queenie only saw them when she took them their meals on trays. They were fallen women, Mrs Waters told her; unmarried ladies who had given in to temptation and were now with child. They were here to have their babes in secret. Queenie wished she could talk to them, but they never looked at her or even thanked her when she said, 'Your supper, ma'am,' or some such thing.

It was late now, gone ten, and the house was silent. It was Queenie's favourite time of the day. Her jobs done, she fetched a plate of cold potatoes and bacon and set herself out a cup and saucer and a pot of tea on the kitchen table. She held her cup by its handle, like a proper lady, and washed down her food with tiny sips. She imagined how the little ones would gawp if they could see her now. Maybe she would go back and show them how well she was doing for herself. One day, she thought. But not just yet. She tried never to think of Mam or Da. Every time she did she saw Mam's eyes, cold and uncaring, as another drunken stranger stood waiting his turn outside their room; and Da slumped drunk in a corner somewhere. So she hung an imaginary sheet across the inside of her head and kept Mam and Da hidden behind it.

Queenie had heard Mrs Waters leave a while ago. She kept strange hours, going out late in the evening and not returning until gone midnight. She often brought a baby back with her, saying she'd met a poor mother on the streets who had begged her to take in her child. The last one had been a feisty little thing with fat red cheeks that had fair hollered the house down. Until Mrs Ellis had dosed it up, that was. It was as quiet as the rest of them now, and as pale. When Mrs Waters had first brought it back with her it had been wearing a beautiful blue velvet cloak and a fine lace bonnet. Mrs Waters had been in high spirits and had sent Queenie out for a bottle of brandy and some hot roast beef. The sisters drank the whole bottle between them then fell to snoring in their chairs while Queenie ate the last of the beef, cold for her supper. She wondered why they had been so pleased with the child. She never saw the cloak and bonnet again, but supposed they had been put away, to be kept nice for when a new home had been found for the babe.

Queenie could hear cockroaches rattling around under the kitchen mats. A sure sign that spring had arrived. She filled a bowl with warmed water from the kettle to wash herself. She undressed and stood in front of the kitchen fire and wiped herself all over with a wet cloth. She rinsed out her drawers and hung them on the fender to dry. They would still be damp by morning, but she only had the one pair and she liked this new feeling of clean. She liked to see the pink of her skin and to smell clean cloth and watch the dirt and dust of the day fly away as she shook out her petticoats and dress. Mrs Ellis had given her the dress, petticoats and underclothing, saying they had belonged to 'one of the young ladies that had been to stay'. The dress was Queenie's pride and joy. It was sky blue with lace trimmings and it swished around her ankles as she went about her work. It had been the best feeling in the world to throw her old dress in with the potato peelings and other kitchen rubbish. She hadn't even wanted to cut it up for cleaning cloths.

Queenie checked on the babies one last time before she went to fetch her mattress. Poor little mites, she thought. All of them unwanted by their mams, Mrs Waters had told her not long after she'd arrived.

'They'd be left for dead on the streets,' she'd said, 'if Mrs Ellis and I didn't take them in. We look after them as best we can until we find someone who does want them.'

Queenie thought the sisters must be do-gooders of some sort. Like the Salvation Army people that Queenie had seen near home sometimes, standing on street corners singing hymns and giving bread to children. The sisters might be a bit odd, thought Queenie, but they'd taken her in at least, and paid good wages too. Queenie thought of the pile of coins hidden in her skirts and promised herself a trip to the fancy goods shop to buy some yellow ribbons for her hair, as soon as she got a day off.

The babies were all lying still as usual, like little marble statues. Most had their eyes closed but a couple were staring into the distance, their eyes half open. They didn't even blink when Queenie put her face to theirs. Queenie wondered sometimes why none of them seemed to be getting any better. Mrs Ellis was very strict with dosing them up with their medicine. She had taught Queenie how to mix it up and now Queenie made a jugful every morning. A piece of builder's lime, as big as her hand, was left to stand for an hour in a quart of water. She would then add a dessertspoonful of the mixture into each of the babies' bottles. 'So the milk doesn't curdle,' Mrs Ellis said. Queenie wasn't allowed to give them the other stuff, mind – *the Quietness*, as Mrs Ellis called it. A foul-smelling liquid from a sticky brown bottle that was kept in Mrs Ellis's pocket.

'Godfrey's Cordial,' Queenie read on the label.

'A drop each morning and night,' Mrs Ellis said, 'and they'll sleep without a murmur.'

Queenie thought that was half the trouble, though; they slept so much they were hardly awake to suckle their bottles. And they were all growing so thin.

'Those children is ill, ain't they ma'am?' she'd said to Mrs Waters.

Mrs Waters had been angry at her. 'Of course they're ill, girl! Little bastards never fare well. But are we not doing the best we can by them? Are there not always full bottles waiting for them? They will feed when they're hungry. They are sickly creatures and with so many of them our nerves can't stand the fussing. Do you want your nights disturbed by their whinings? I would think not indeed. It is a mother's blessing, *the Quietness*, a mother's blessing.'

Queenie didn't mention it again; after all, Mrs Waters must know best.

There were only six babies on the sofa now. Mrs Waters had taken some of them away. 'To healthy homes in the country,' she'd told Queenie.

'Not long for the rest of you,' Queenie whispered. 'Mrs Waters'll find you new mams too, I'm sure of it.'

Queenie lay on her mattress and pulled a blanket over. It still felt strange having a bed to herself. Sometimes she missed the little ones snuggled into her and their snufflings and coughs. It was lonely on the kitchen floor, with the dwindling fire throwing strange shadows on the walls and lighting up the cobwebbed corners of the room. The silence hurt her ears. No squabbling neighbours or drunken cater-wauling, no dogs barking or cats screeching. Nothing, not even the sound of another's breath. She closed her eyes and wished one of the babies would stir. Just so she wouldn't feel so alone.

18

Ellen

'What are those marks?' asked Mary the following morning as she helped me dress.

'What marks?' I replied. Although I knew exactly the marks she meant. I had felt the grip of Jacob's fingers on my skin all through the night. Now the bruises must be showing.

'Your shoulders, miss. They're black and blue,' said Mary.

I sat heavily into my chair.

'Oh, it is nothing,' I said. 'I fell from my bed in the night.'

I was ashamed of my lie, but more ashamed of the truth. Unwanted tears pricked at my eyes. I felt empty inside and desperate to see Jacob. He had not meant to hurt me, I was sure. Mary was looking at me, her eyes full of concern. I put my arms around her waist and buried my head in her soft stomach. Only Mary has ever truly loved me, I thought.

She smoothed my hair. 'There now,' she said. 'All will be well.'

A great shouting noise suddenly came from downstairs and made us pull apart. Mary frowned and went to open my bedroom door. Father's voice rose up to us, loud and angry.

'You will leave this house today, boy! I will not be threatened again! Be gone when I get back!'

I looked at Mary and whispered, 'Jacob?' Something crashed, a door banged and then Jacob's voice.

'Go to hell! I will ruin you! See if I don't!'

I jumped from my chair and went to run downstairs.

'No, miss!' warned Mary. 'You are in your dressing gown! Stay here. Let things calm down.'

'But I need to go to him! He cannot leave! Oh, what has happened, Mary?'

'I don't know, miss. But I think it best if you don't interfere.' She went to the window and pulled the curtains to one side. 'Your father has just left in the carriage.'

'Then I must go and see Jacob straight away!'

'No, please, miss! I don't think you should get involved.'

'But I *am* involved! I love him, Mary. He is the most wonderful thing that has ever happened to me. I cannot just let him leave! I *have* to go to him.'

'Then at least finish your dress, miss. Please.'

I sighed. 'Well hurry, then!' I stood and let her lace me up. Then I stepped into my petticoats and gown and tapped my foot impatiently as she fastened the buttons at the back.

'There,' she said. 'Just your hair now.'

'My hair will be fine as it is,' I snapped. 'I must go!'

I rushed out of the door and lifted my skirts to run along the corridor and down the stairs. One of the housemaids was kneeling on the hallway floor sweeping up the broken remains of a vase. I ran past her into the dining room. It

84

was empty. I went to the drawing room next. It smelt of father's cigars, but it too was empty. He must be in the library, I thought. I slowed down and took a deep breath before I opened the door. A fire had been lit in the grate and the room was warm and expectant. It was my favourite room. The hundreds of whispering books which lined the walls from floor to ceiling had been my only friends. Until Jacob. But there was no sign of him.

I stopped for a moment and thought of how he had first touched me by the window. That soft, lemon-scented touch that had made me feel I was not alone for the first time in my life. He could not leave! I had to find him.

I ran back out to the hallway. The housemaid was just gathering up her brushes. 'Have you seen Master Grey?' I asked her. 'Has he gone back to his room?'

'No, miss,' she said. 'He went out into the garden a while back.'

'Has a carriage been ordered?'

'No, miss, I don't think so.'

He could not be leaving immediately, then. I would have time to find him and talk to him and persuade him to apologise to Father for whatever had caused the upset. It would be all right. He would not go. Besides, he had nowhere else to go to.

The garden was shiny with the spring dew of morning and the bottom of my skirts grew damp as I hurried across the lawn. The sun was still pale in the sky, the air not yet warm. I wished I had brought my shawl. I knew where he would be and I could not get there quickly enough. There was the stone archway. I ran the last few steps, ducked under the archway and into the flower garden. He was there. Sitting on our bench with his head in his hands.

'Jacob,' I breathed. 'Oh, Jacob, I have been looking everywhere for you.'

He sat still, not even lifting his head.

'Jacob,' I said again. 'I have been so scared. You will not leave, will you? You will make better what has come between you and Father?'

His shoulders began to shake. He was crying. I could not bear it. I knelt down to put my arms about him. Then he looked up at me. I saw he was not crying. He was laughing. I pulled away and stood up. I was confused.

'Is . . . is everything all right, Jacob? Have I been worried for no reason?'

He stood and smiled at me and I smiled back. Then he held his arms out to me. I moved towards him and he wrapped them tight around me. I relaxed into him.

'Oh, Jacob,' I murmured.

His arms grew tighter around me. My face was buried in his chest. It was becoming hard to breathe so I tried to twist my head to one side. Jacob gripped tighter. He bent his head to my ear and I could feel his warm breath.

'You stupid girl!' he hissed.

My heart stopped.

'Do you really believe I ever felt anything for you? You are nothing. Less than nothing.'

I tried to pull away to see his face. To see if he was making fun of me. But he held me there. I could feel his heart beating steadily. Strong and loud.

'Why do you think I came here? Because I *wanted* to?' He laughed. Then his voice grew fierce.

'Do you think I wanted to come *begging* to the man who betrayed Mother? The great Dr William Swift, who is held in such esteem by society? Such a great man he would not even help his own *sister* when she needed it.'

'Please, Jacob!' I pleaded. My voice sounded muffled and strange. I did not understand what he was saying.

'I only came here to get what is rightfully mine. To have a taste of the kind of life that should have been mine and Mother's.'

I managed to turn my head and take a deep breath.

'I do not understand,' I said, my voice shaking. 'Father has taken you in. You have that life now.'

'What? A life among the dead? Cutting off limbs and weighing organs? Spending my days in that room of death? I don't want to *work*, you foolish girl!'

Jacob stroked my hair. For a brief moment I thought all would be well. He does not know what he is saying, I thought. He misses his mother. Then suddenly he grasped my hair and pulled my head back. I cried out in pain. He stared at me. His face was twisted and ugly. His eyes were black.

'You have no idea how you have ruined my life.' His words fell like drops of poison. 'If *you* had never been born, Mother and your *dear* father would never have argued. She didn't agree with him, you see. She thought what he was doing was so very wrong. So she left, and he washed his hands of her.'

Jacob let go of my hair and pulled me close again with

one arm around my waist. His other hand was sliding down my back and on to my skirts. He was pulling and bunching up the fabric. I tried to call for Mary but all that came out was a sob. My head was spinning. Why was Jacob saying these things? Why was he doing this to me?

'I know your father's dirty secret, Ellen. That's why I came. To ask him for money in exchange for his reputation. But what did he do? Persuaded me to become his apprentice. Said it would bring me far greater riches in the end. Stupidly I agreed.'

Jacob was still tugging my skirts and I could feel his hand through my petticoat, pressing on the back of my thigh.

'Jacob,' I managed to say. 'What . . . what are you doing?' My heart was throbbing in my head.

'It didn't take me long to realise that your father had taken me for a fool. Shutting me in that room day after day with no company but corpses. I am worth more than that!'

He pulled hard at my petticoat and I heard the thin muslin rip. I struggled to free myself, gasping with the effort. His grip on me tightened.

'Jacob! Please!' I begged. 'Let me go!' I closed my eyes and wished for it all to be a nightmare. I wished to be anywhere but here. I felt the morning breeze on the back of my neck and I heard the chirrup of a goldfinch in the distance. These things from the normal world calmed me for a moment. Then Jacob's voice came again.

'So I told him, Ellen. I told him I wanted only money. A modest amount. Then I would be on my way and his little secret would be safe.'

Jacob pulled me to the ground.

'No!' I screamed.

His hand covered my mouth and my heart beat so violently I felt the ground beneath me shake. He pushed his face into mine. I whined in terror.

'He is not a man to be threatened, is he Ellen? It seems he doesn't want me here any more. He thinks I can do him no harm. Someone like me ruin the reputation of the great William Swift?'

Jacob rolled on top of me and I knew I was lost. I lay perfectly still and tried to disappear into the ground. The dew on the grass was cold on the bare skin of my legs.

'I will tell the world his dirty secret. I will tell the world all about you. Ellen Swift. Not the daughter of Eliza and William Swift. No . . . you are *nothing*, Ellen. The bastard of a maid. An ordinary, simple maid that your father liked the look of.'

A bastard. The word filled my head. I closed my eyes. My head was heavy. My legs were heavy. Jacob was heavy on top of me.

'Do you think your father did it to your whore of a mother like this, Ellen? Just like this?'

There was a sharp pain deep inside me. I gasped and clenched my fists. I felt tears rolling down my cheeks. Jacob moved inside me, faster and faster.

I thought of Father plunging his hands into the dead man's body, and I felt like a corpse lying on a cold marble slab with all my most private secrets exposed to the world.

Jacob stiffened and sighed and pushed himself away from me. I kept my eyes shut tight and I heard him cough and the swish of his footsteps on the wet grass. The goldfinch was still singing and I listened to it until all was still.

19

Queenie

Queenie woke with a start. She stared into the darkness of the kitchen wondering what had woken her. There was not a sound from the sofa. Maybe one of the babies had whimpered, but had now gone back to sleep? She reached out for her candle and the matches. She'd best check that all was well.

The candlelight flickered over the small faces and Queenie watched closely for each little chest to rise and fall. They seemed peaceful enough now. Maybe one had had a bad dream. Queenie remembered how Mam would sing lullabies to the little ones if they woke in the night. She began to hum softly as she tucked blankets round the babies.

'Soft the drowsy hours are creeping, hill and dale in slumber sleeping, I my loved one's watch am keeping, all through the night.'

The words drifted through her head. She paused as she came to the last baby in the row, then looked back and counted. One, two, three, four, five. Only five of them? But there had been six there when she'd gone to bed. Then she heard a noise, a rustling sound coming from the scullery. She froze. The sound came nearer. Then the kitchen door began to slowly open. Queenie swallowed a scream.

'What are you doing, girl?'

Queenie caught her breath. It was just Mrs Waters carrying a lit candle stump and still with her cloak and bonnet on. She had a brown paper parcel tucked under her arm.

'Was just checking on the babes, ma'am. Thought I heard one of 'em crying.'

'They are all peaceful now, are they?'

'Yes, ma'am. But ma'am, there's only the five of 'em now. Were six when I went to bed, ma'am.'

'Well, that's because one has been fetched away to a new home. It's all been arranged. The carriage has just left.'

'Oh, ma'am. I see. And has it gone to a healthy place in the country, ma'am? Like the others?'

'Yes, yes. A healthy place in the country. Now I must get my rest. See that I am not disturbed in the morning. If you need anything, then speak to Mrs Ellis.'

'Yes, ma'am.'

'Goodnight, Queenie.'

'Goodnight, Mrs Waters.'

Queenie went back to her mattress and lay down. She was wide awake now, her head spinning with questions. She heard a bang in the distance. It sounded like the front door. But it couldn't be. Mrs Waters wouldn't be going out again. She was off to bed, she'd said so herself.

Queenie wondered why Mrs Waters hadn't woken her to help get the baby ready, and how she'd managed to be so quiet about it. She hoped she'd wrapped it up well. It would be cold for a small thing out at night. And what was she doing in the scullery? There was only the washtub in there for the dishes and the laundry, and the mops and brushes for cleaning. Maybe she'd been looking for string for her parcel? But the post office wouldn't be open till morning. Couldn't it have waited? She was a strange one all right, thought Queenie. A very strange one. But at least another baby had a home to go to. Queenie imagined it cradled in its new mam's arms, lulled to sleep by the rocking carriage carrying it away to a healthy place in the country.

Mrs Ellis was down in the kitchen early. Queenie had changed the babies' napkins and put the dirty ones in to soak. The kitchen fire was blazing and she had laid the breakfast trays out.

'Fetch me a bowl of warm water and some clean cloths!' ordered Mrs Ellis. 'One of our young ladies has gone into labour. Quickly, girl! Bring them up to me. The front bedroom at the top.' She hurried out of the room, rolling her sleeves up as she went.

Queenie ran to the scullery to fetch the big enamel bowl and a pile of old sheeting she had being cutting down for napkins. As she picked up the cloths she noticed the kitchen scissors lying on the side and some scraps of brown paper. So Mrs Waters had wrapped her parcel in here? Queenie didn't have the chance to wonder why as she hurried to fill the bowl with water from the kettle.

As she carried the bowl carefully up two flights of stairs, minding not to spill a drop of water, she could hear cries and groans getting louder and louder. The door to the front bedroom was ajar and she pushed it open with her shoulder.

'On the table here.' Mrs Ellis gestured her to put the

bowl down. The young lady on the bed was groaning deeply. Her eyes were wide with terror and her hands were twisting the sheets round and round like a mad thing.

'God help me! God help me!' she screamed.

'Now, now,' said Mrs Ellis. 'There's no need for all this fuss. The baby's coming whether you like it or not, and shrieking like that won't make it come any quicker.'

Queenie thought the lady looked so small and helpless lying there in the centre of the bed. With her nightdress pushed up around her thighs and her fair hair loose and sticking to the sweat on her forehead, she looked like a young girl; nothing like the quiet lady of the past few weeks in her flowing gowns with her hair piled high on her head. Queenie wanted to tell her it would be all right. She'd seen Mam do it all well enough and knew the pain would quickly end as soon as the lady had her baby in her arms.

'Don't just stand there gawping, girl! Fetch Mrs Waters!' Mrs Ellis turned away from Queenie and bent down to peer between the lady's legs.

'Yes, ma'am,' said Queenie and she hurried out of the room. She jumped as she almost bumped into the other young lady, the dark-haired one. She was standing right outside the door, still wearing her nightgown and looking as pale as a ghost.

'Is she dying?' she whispered to Queenie.

'Dying? No, ma'am. No. She's not dying. The baby's coming is all.'

'I know the baby's coming,' hissed the lady. 'But is it killing her?'

'No, ma'am. It's just the pain. There's no harm. It'll be over soon. It's how it always is with babies.'

To her horror, the lady burst into tears and grabbed hold of Queenie's arms. 'Can't you make it go away?' she cried. 'Please make it go away. I can't do that. I can't! Oh God! I am ruined, I am ruined!'

Just then there was a wail from the bedroom behind them. A low quivering wail that got louder and stronger and deeper. Queenie and the lady stood in silence. The wail got louder and louder and grew into a roar of agony. Then it suddenly stopped and Queenie realised she was holding her breath and the lady's fingers were digging into her skin.

Then a small tinny sound broke through the quiet and Queenie shook off the lady's fingers and said, 'See, baby's here all safe now.' The lady was trembling and crying gently now, but before Queenie could steer her back to her room, Mrs Waters appeared at the top of the stairs.

'Miss Godfrey! You really shouldn't be upsetting yourself in your condition. Back to your room now, and I'll have Queenie bring you up some tea.' She glared at Queenie as she led the lady away.

Later that evening Mrs Ellis brought the newborn babe down to the kitchen and told Queenie to make it up a feed. It was mewling gently, its little face all wrinkled and screwed up.

'Can I hold it?' asked Queenie.

'I don't see why not,' said Mrs Ellis. 'But don't make a habit of it. We don't want it spoiling.'

The baby pushed its face into Queenie's chest, its mouth

searching for its mam's titty. Queenie wriggled the rubber teat into its mouth and the baby pulled on it hard. She had fetched the milk from the dairy only a while ago, so knew it was fresh and creamy. She hadn't watered it down with builder's lime, even though Mrs Ellis always insisted on it. It didn't seem right to somehow, with the little one being only a few hours old. She held the baby close. Its head smelt of warm biscuits and honey. A strange feeling rushed through Queenie's body and she found herself hoping that this baby stayed well.

20

Ellen

The sun was warm now. I rolled onto my side and curled into myself. My cheek rested on the grass. It smelt of wet soil. I had pulled my skirts down to cover myself and glimpsed a smudge of blood on my petticoats. I tried not to think of it. I tried not to think of anything. I wanted to stay there forever; curled up on the soft grass with just the distant rumble of noises you can only hear when you are still and hardly breathing. I stared at the buttercup in front of my eyes. It was so close that when I blew gently, it trembled. I closed my eyes and the buttercup stayed as a fuzzy white shape on the insides of my eyelids.

'Oh, miss! Oh, miss! What's happened?'

Suddenly Mary was there. She touched my shoulder gently; felt my face. 'Did you faint, miss? Shall I call the doctor out?'

I opened my eyes and looked at her face, which was creased with concern. I couldn't speak.

'Do you think you can get up, miss? Least let's try and get you back to the house.'

She gently lifted me to sit. 'Just rest there a minute, miss, and get your bearings. Oh! You have blood on your . . .' She stopped and began to pick out crushed buttercups that were tangled in my hair. 'Now, let's get you up. Come on. Lean on me and we'll take it slowly.'

I clung to her arm. Her familiar smell of clean laundry and her soothing voice made me want to cry. But I knew if I started, I would never stop. We walked back up the garden. Mary talked nonsense all the way.

'If this warm weather keeps up, miss, we'll be having to do the spring cleaning early, I'm sure. Maybe we can get your mother out in the garden this year?'

I wanted to tell her what had happened, but I did not have the words. As we got nearer to the house I stopped. I did not want to go on. I looked at Mary. Her face was drained of colour.

'What is it, miss?' she asked.

'Jacob?' I said in a whisper.

Mary's voice was hard. 'He's gone, miss. Now let's get you to your room before anyone sees the state you're in.'

I realised then that I would not have to find the words. Mary already knew.

Mary undressed me. Bathed me and took away my ruined underclothes. I made her swear to tell no one. She asked no questions. She let it be known that I was unwell with a chill; that I would need a few days' bed rest. Mother came to my room only once. She walked to the side of my bed and looked at me silently. I looked back at her, and then she left. My mother, who was not my mother.

Jacob was not mentioned. I did not know where he had gone and I did not want to ask. It was as though he had never really existed. He was a dream and a nightmare all at once.

My heart was frozen solid and I did not think I would ever heal.

I knew now why Mother despised me. Why she could hardly bear to look at me. I was the daughter of a maid. An ordinary, simple maid who bore Father a child when she could not.

I was nothing.

I understood now why I had never been loved. Even my real mother cannot have loved me, to leave me as she did.

I *was* nothing. I had nothing. Only Mary.

The days passed. Empty and heavy. I left my bed and spent long hours sewing. I took my meals in the dining room again. The food was tasteless. I was becoming more and more invisible. I felt sure Father and Mother would not notice if I disappeared altogether.

There was only Mary.

I watched her going about her duties and listened to her chattering her nonsense. She was the one who had cared for me all my life. She was the one who was always there for me. She had never let me down. I looked at her closely. An idea began to grow in my head. A warm idea that spread through me and started to thaw the ice that Jacob had left in my heart.

21

Queenie

The weather had grown warmer. Queenie hung washed napkins out in the yard to dry instead of round the fire. She let the kitchen door open so the air could circle in and push out the smells of sick babies and stale cooking. Out in the back yard there was nothing but a couple of old chairs. Weeds grew through cracks in the yard wall and grass pushed its way through the brick paving. It smelt sweet outside, though, and the fresh air seemed to blow a weight off Queenie's shoulders.

It would do the babies good, she thought, to get out for a while. Since she'd arrived at Wild Street she couldn't remember any of them having been moved from the sofa. Queenie dragged her mattress from the scullery and laid it out in the yard under the shade of an overgrown bush. Then she fetched the babies one by one and arranged them in a neat row. She pulled loose the blankets and assortment of linens that swaddled the tiny bodies, so they could feel the air between their fingers and toes. They all lay still as could be. Even so, Queenie swore she could see a faint colour seeping into their cheeks.

Satisfied they were all safe, Queenie brought out a knife, a bowl of water and a handful of potatoes to peel. She settled on one of the chairs and began to work. There was a mewl from the mattress. Queenie looked up and saw that the newest baby was awake, waving its arms and legs in the air. Queenie had named her Little Lady Rose on account of having a real lady for a mam and because the pink blanket her mam had left for her was as soft as a rose petal and was edged in silk. She never let on to the sisters, though. It was a secret between her and Rose.

Queenie smiled to see Little Rose grabbing at the invisible air. Her thighs and arms still had rings of fat on them. Queenie thought of the day Rose had been born in the bedroom at the top and how her mam had left the very next day. Slipping away without ever saying goodbye to her baby. Rose had been hungrier than the other babies to begin with. Sometimes Queenie gave her an extra feed in the night with milk she had kept to one side. Rose had been noisier than the rest too and Mrs Waters had shouted at her a couple of times to 'shut the whining pest up!'

But Rose had grown a lot quieter of late. With Mrs Ellis giving her regular doses of *the Quietness*, Rose slept almost as much as the other babies. Queenie was glad to see her awake now. At least she had seen the outside and felt the sun on her skin.

'Queenie!' Mrs Ellis's voice came from inside the house. 'Queenie!' Her voice rose to a high shrill. Queenie jumped from her chair, knocking over the bowl of water and half the peeled potatoes. As she bent to pick them up, Mrs Ellis appeared at the kitchen door.

'What do you think you are doing? Are you mad, girl?' She ran over to the mattress and piled three of the babies in her arms. 'Bring the other three!' she ordered. 'Quick now!'

Queenie picked up the tiny bodies and followed Mrs Ellis back into the kitchen.

Mrs Ellis whirled round. 'DON'T YOU EVER DO THAT AGAIN!'

Queenie gulped hard. 'But ma'am, I only thought the fresh air would do 'em good.'

'Maybe it would and maybe it wouldn't. That is no concern of yours.'

'I'm sorry, ma'am. I didn't know I was doing something wrong.'

Mrs Ellis shut the back door with a bang. 'We want no gossip or people sticking their noses in our business. You keep those babies away from prying eyes.'

'Yes, ma'am,' said Queenie quietly. You old cow, she thought. What harm was there in the babies getting fresh air? Being cooped up all day just wasn't right.

Mrs Ellis's face softened. 'Well now, I'm glad you understand me, Queenie. Best we keep this quiet, eh? No point in bothering Mrs Waters with it all.'

'No, ma'am,' said Queenie. She placed her armful of babies back on the sofa and tucked in their blankets. Little Rose had gone back to sleep. She looked so pretty wrapped in her pink blanket. Queenie ran the back of her finger across the baby's cheek. It felt so tender and soft and unspoilt. She stood and turned. Mrs Ellis was watching her, a strange look on her face.

'I'll get back to me jobs now then, ma'am,' said Queenie.

'Just a minute,' said Mrs Ellis. She rummaged in her

apron pockets and brought out a handful of coins. 'Your wages, Queenie. Here. And a little extra too. We're pleased with your work. You're fitting in nicely.'

'Oh. Thank you, ma'am.'

'And why don't you take the afternoon off? You've been here long enough now to deserve one.'

'Truly, ma'am?'

Mrs Ellis nodded.

'Well I will, then. Thank you, ma'am!'

'Just be back in time for the evening feeds.'

'Yes, ma'am. Course, ma'am.'

Queenie hurried out, all thoughts of the babies disappearing from her head as she listened to the coins jingling in her pocket.

It was strange being back out on the streets. Apart from fetching milk from the dairy on the corner of the road, Queenie hadn't left Wild Street once. It was hard to decide what to do first. She was dizzy with the freedom of it all. She had more money in her pocket than she had ever seen before. She wanted to skip with excitement. For a brief second a picture of Mam and the little ones appeared in her head. Mam with her sleeves rolled up beating dust out of a blanket and the little ones sitting on a step somewhere, in the sunshine. No, sod them, she thought. She pushed the picture away. Today was for her. She had worked hard, she deserved it.

22

Ellen

'And how are you today, miss?' asked Mary as she bustled into my room with my breakfast tray. 'It's a beautiful day. Maybe you would fancy a stroll in the garden later?'

I shook my head. The thought of fresh air and birdsong and the mocking yellow of buttercups on the lawn filled me with loathing. I had not been able to look out of the window since that day and preferred the curtains to be kept closed. But I knew Mary would be so happy to see me take some air. To see some colour back in my cheeks.

'Mary,' I said. I was nervous and tried to keep my voice from shaking. 'Please come and sit by me for a moment.' I patted my bed.

'Of course, miss. What is it?'

She sat beside me and I reached for her hand. The warm roughness of her skin soothed me and I took a deep breath.

'I know the truth, Mary.'

'The truth, miss? What truth is that?'

'Jacob told me,' I said, looking at her dear face. 'Jacob told me that I am not my mother's child.'

Mary went still. Her face seemed to crumple and she gripped my hand tight.

'You knew, didn't you?' I said. 'You have always known.'

'Oh, miss,' she said softly. 'I am so sorry. I am so sorry I was never able to tell you. I thought it was for the best.'

'Best for who, Mary?' I looked at her face for clues. For any guilt or shame in her eyes. There was nothing but concern.

'Best for you, miss, of course. What good would it have done for you to have known?'

'To have known I was a *bastard*, do you mean? That I was nothing?'

'No, miss, no! Don't say that!'

'Well, it is true, isn't it? That is why Jacob did what he did to me! To punish me for having all this when I am a nobody!'

'That *boy*,' Mary spat out the word, 'is nothing but an evil monster! Do you hear me? A monster! Don't you ever say you are a nobody, miss! It's not true!'

I had never seen Mary cry before. The tears that filled the creases under her eyes seemed to take her by surprise and she hastily brought up her apron to dab them away. I put my hand out to her, waiting for her to say more; wanting her to tell me what I was thinking. I willed her to tell me. She took a deep breath and I leaned towards her. But instead of saying the words I needed to hear, she kissed me quickly on the top of my head, rose from my bed and hurried out of the room.

I fell back on to my pillows; confused and frustrated but strangely elated to have seen Mary cry because of me. I would have to be patient with her. She would tell me in time. I knew she would.

I closed my eyes. I was so very, very weary. There was a

foreign taste on my tongue that I could not get rid of. It had appeared over the last few days and no matter how many times I rinsed my mouth with peppermint water, it would not go. There was a constant nausea in my belly too, that had only this morning caused me to vomit last night's dinner of ham and rice pudding.

I lay on my bed. Too tired even to cry. I was sore all over. Even my breasts were heavy and tender. That at least was a familiar feeling. A sign that my monthly bleed was due. I lay there counting the days and then the weeks. I became muddled in my head and began to count again. Could it truly have been that long? I counted again. The terrible memory of Jacob pushing into me came flooding into my mind.

My heart was beating wildly as I realised that my monthly bleed had not come. Father's words rang loud in my ears.

Any irregularities can only lead to hysteria or in the very worst of cases – insanity.

After all that had happened to me, was I to go insane now?

I sat up, trembling and feeling faint. There was another possibility as to why my bleed had not come, I realised. A possibility that filled me with the most cold and dreadful fear.

23

Queenie

It was a perfect afternoon. The air was warm; the sky spread with clouds. Queenie could almost hear Mam saying, *There's plenty enough blue to make a pair of sailor's trousers!* Queenie turned right out of Wild Street and made her way to Drury Lane. She walked past the theatres and noisy taverns and found herself on Long Acre. Everywhere there was hustle and bustle and noise. The streets were full of gentlemen going about their business, in and out of the varnish maker's and coach maker's shops. There were ladies with baskets of neatly wrapped parcels, flower girls with wilting posies and shopkeepers shouting their wares. Horses and cabs trundled up and down the road sending up clouds of dust. Children played outside shops. Queenie could smell coffee, burnt sugar and the warm, sweet stench of horse dung. She bought a cake from a baker's and broke off lumps of the buttery pastry to eat as she wandered along.

She heard laughter and clapping and saw a crowd gathered on a corner. Queenie pushed her way through. An old man, dressed in underclothes, she thought, was standing with a long pole in one hand and a basin in the other. 'Ladies and gentlemen!' he shouted. 'Throw your coppers in here and you shall witness feats of such strength and dexterity you would never have believed possible!'

Coins jangled into his basin and the old man bowed and put it on the ground. Queenie watched as the old man stuck the end of the pole into his waistband so the length of it waved high above the crowd. A boy appeared from behind him, dressed in a similar fashion. He took a bow, then jumped and grabbed hold of the pole. Queenie gasped as the boy seemed to run up the pole while the old man balanced it in his waistband. The boy held on to the end of the pole with one hand then slowly turned upside down and waved with his free hand. The crowd roared. Queenie cheered, caught up in the happy mood.

She watched as the boy jumped back to the ground and more coins were thrown into the basin. The old man put his arm around the boy and hugged him. They were father and son, thought Queenie. The old man smiled a wide, toothless smile. Queenie saw the pride shining in his eyes and knew at once how much he loved his son. Suddenly she felt alone, even amongst the crowd. She wanted to tell someone what she'd seen. Tally would have loved it. He'd never seen anything like that before.

She looked at the people around her, still gawping at the old man. He'd stuck a wooden tumbler to his head and was catching brightly coloured balls that his son was throwing in the air. Queenie turned away and began to push her way back on to the street. She was mad at herself. She wished she'd never stopped to look. What was the point in seeing such a sight if there was no one to share it with?

She walked fast to the end of the street, and then the entire length of another. A carriage pulled up in front of her, and a woman wearing long satin gloves and a veil stepped out and hurried into the shop opposite. Queenie wandered over and peered into the shop window. It was a milliners; the inside stuffed with hats of all types, decorated with feathers, fruits and flowers. The lady was sitting in a chair. Two assistants hovered around her. Queenie wondered what the lady's new hat would be like. She wondered what it would be like to sit in a chair like that and have assistants to bring you whatever you chose, because they knew you had the money to pay for it. Queenie had never been in a shop before. Not one like that, anyway. They would boot her out before she got over the threshold. She felt the coins in her pocket. She would find a fancy shop, she decided, brimming with ribbons and lace. She would go inside and choose the prettiest thing she could see.

Across the road from Charing Cross Station Queenie saw people milling about in front of the entrance to a passageway. Over the top of the entrance was a sign painted in gold. *Lowther Arcade*. Queenie walked inside and stopped, amazed by the sight that met her eyes. The passageway was lined with shops; the whole thing covered by a roof of glass. Shafts of sunlight poured down and fell on piles of treasure that spilled out of every shop doorway. The air was so light and bright and the whole place hummed with noise: the rustle of dresses, the clatter of feet and the echo of voices and laughter. There were tables laden with bracelets, hair ornaments, brooches and rings with stones as big as eggs. Queenie walked slowly along, putting her hand out to stroke a gleaming wooden horse. She stopped to gaze in wonder at a miniature house, its front open and each room furnished with tiny tables, chairs and beds. Every shop had something different: walking sticks, perfume bottles, china dolls, cakes of soap, candlesticks and fans. Queenie had walked into a whole new world and she never wanted to leave it. After a long while she chose to buy a cake of pink soap. It smelt of roses. The shopkeeper wrapped it in a square of brown paper and tied it with string. Next Queenie bought a length of ribbon, as yellow and glossy as a pat of fresh butter. The ribbon was folded neatly into a sheet of silver tissue.

It had been so easy. The shopkeepers had smiled at her and thanked her for her custom. They had treated her like a lady. She clutched her parcels tight as she made her way back to Wild Street. They felt like the most precious things in the world.

24

Ellen

I rang for Mary. I needed her now like I had never needed her before. With this terrible fear coursing through me, I could not be patient any longer. I tried to calm myself as I waited for her to arrive. I got out of bed and paced the room. It was all so familiar: my dressing table, my wash stand, my armchair, my wardrobe. All of it, the paper on the walls and the painting of a rose-filled garden hanging over the fireplace, had been there my whole life. It was so familiar that I went about my days taking no notice of it all. It was the same with Mary, I realised. She too had been there my whole life too. She was as familiar and as invisible to me as my bedroom furniture.

'Yes, miss?' Mary poked her head around the bedroom door. 'You rang?'

'Mary . . .' I took a deep breath. 'Come in and close the door.' She did as I asked. I could see by the blotches on her face that she had not long stopped crying. 'Mary.' I swallowed hard. 'Now that Jacob has told me the truth about myself, I want you to know that I am glad. I am glad I know the truth and I am glad that it is you.'

Mary looked puzzled. 'What is me, miss?'

I hesitated. I thought she had understood me. 'I . . . I

am so glad it is you, Mary. I am so glad you are my mother.'

Mary's hand flew to her mouth and she sat heavily in my armchair. 'Your mother? Miss! Whatever makes you think such a thing?'

I stared at her. My heart was thumping in my ears. 'But you *are* my mother, aren't you? It can only be you. Please tell me it is you!' Why wouldn't she say it? Couldn't she see how much I needed her to tell me the truth?

She stood up and grabbed my hands. 'Miss, I am not your mother. Believe you me, I am not. But if I had a daughter I would wish her to be just like you. Oh, miss, this awful business truly has left you at sixes and sevens.'

'You are lying!' I shouted. Did she think I was going insane? I felt my face grow hot with shame and anger. 'Jacob said my mother was a maid. Here in this house. And you have been here all my life. Who else can it be?'

'Oh, miss! It is true. Your mother was a maid here. But *another* maid. Not me.'

I did not want to believe it was true. I wanted Mary to be my mother. Tears filled my eyes. I needed to belong to her. To belong to someone who loved me. Mary did love me, didn't she? I pulled away from her. Maybe she was just doing her duty. She cared for Mother and Father too, after all. Had I mistaken her diligence for love?

'If you are not my mother,' I shouted, 'then who was she?' My voice was brittle with anger. I hated Mary at that moment. 'WHO WAS MY MOTHER?'

Mary lowered her head. 'I never knew her, miss. Least

not properly. She left a couple of months after I came. When you were just a newborn.'

'She left me?' I whispered. 'Why? Why did she do that?'

'Oh, miss,' Mary said gently. 'She had no choice. How could she have looked after you on her own? She was just a maid.'

'But why could she not have stayed?'

'Think of the scandal, miss! Your father would have been ruined. Your mother . . . Mrs Swift, I mean, could never seem to keep a baby inside her for long, as you know. You were the answer. You were the child they needed. Your real mother knew you'd be best off here.'

'How do you know all this?' I asked suddenly. Mary's face clouded with guilt.

'Oh, miss,' Mary pleaded. 'Don't be angry with me. I always thought it was for the best. I helped bring you into the world, you know? And your Father . . . well, he paid me to keep quiet and promised me a job for life. It was for the best, miss, believe me it was for the best.'

'Aunt Isabella did not think so did she? She hated Father for what he did and she probably HATED YOU TOO! Don't you see it would have been better if I had not been born at all!'

Mary flinched. She looked at the floor. She suddenly looked old and worn out. I hoped that she was feeling some pain. She deserved to.

A sad silence filled the room. But I could not stop myself from thinking and wondering.

'What was she like?' I asked.

Mary looked directly at me. 'She was beautiful, miss.

Thick black hair and dancing eyes. Green as green, they were. But quiet, she was. Quiet and sad.'

'And what was her name?'

'Dolly, miss. Her name was Dolly.'

So now I knew. I knew why I had never belonged. I knew why I had never been loved. I was kept here to protect Father's good name. To give him the respectability of a family. To save him from the embarrassment of a barren wife.

The day passed in a haze. I would not speak to Mary. I could not even look at her. She had known all along that I was no better than her. She had pretended all my life. I felt completely hollow; my insides scooped out and discarded. Everything I had ever known was all pretence, but it somehow all made sense now.

I thought of Dolly with her dark hair and green eyes. Did I look like her? I wondered. Where was she now? Did she ever think of me? I would go to Father, I resolved. I would confront him with the truth. Demand for him to find my mother. To bring her back. But even as I thought these things my stomach lurched with fright. What good would it do? He would never risk his reputation. He would put me out on the streets. Then where would I go? What would I do?

I sat in the library. The door leading to the garden was ajar and a faint smell of grass and rain drifted inside. The thought of outside still made me feel queer, but I forced myself to stay. I had searched the bookshelves for a particular book that I had once stumbled upon and read with horrified fascination. I had it now, open on my lap: *A Treatise on the Diseases of Married Females.*

Mary came in. She tiptoed around; straightening cushions and tidying up my tea things. My silence did not stop her from speaking.

'I know it's been a shock, miss. A terrible, terrible shock. All of it. But you know Dolly would not have coped with you out there on her own. Who would have given her a job with a baby in tow? You wouldn't even have got a place in the workhouse together. And you've had a good home here. More than most people could ever wish for.'

'I do not need you in here, Mary. Please go,' I said abruptly.

'As you wish, miss.' She clamped her lips together and picked up my tray to leave. 'But just so as you know,' she said in a low voice. 'Your father has been enquiring on your time of the month. So you will have to allow me to come to your room later to collect up your soiled cloths.'

She walked out and the true horror of my situation brought a half moan, half cry from deep inside me. Trying to control my panic, I bent my head to the book again. Strange words and expressions swam before my eyes: *conjugal relations, encumbered with child, parturition, fecundation, lactation, conception.* I put the book down again. It all made sense. But it could not be.

I was unwell with the horror of all that had happened, I told myself. I was fatigued and my imagination was inflamed. I jumped from my chair and hastily put the book back in its place. Then I wiped my hands on my skirts as though they had been dirtied.

The sun was lighting up the garden and shining through the windows. My chair was standing in a puddle of warmth. I sat back down in it. Tiredness swept over me again; in my toes and limbs and head, and in the pit of my stomach. I closed my eyes and let the warmth of the sun creep into my bones.

I dreamt of Jacob and of a beautiful dark-haired woman walking by his side. I was watching from the window of a dusty attic room as they strolled down the garden arm in arm. Jacob picked her a red rose. He pinned it to her gown and it looked like a splash of blood against the emerald-green silk. I watched them walk further into the distance. Then they disappeared. I banged my fists against the window and shouted their names. *Mother! Jacob!* But they could not hear me.

When I woke the sun had gone in. I sat in the quiet of the room and listened to my heat thumping in my throat. I had never felt so alone.

Mary came into my bedroom early the next morning and placed a glass of toast water on my bedside table. 'Drink this,' she said. 'You've been looking very peaky of late. It will do you good.'

I looked at the brown water. I could smell its warm yeastiness and my stomach heaved.

'I know you don't wish to speak to me,' continued Mary, 'but I must follow your father's orders.' She looked around my room. 'Now, where are your soiled cloths? Your father is waiting to inspect them.'

My stomach heaved again. I leaned over the side of my

bed and pulled my chamber pot out from under it. My stomach rose and sour liquid poured from my mouth into the pot. Mary came to me at once. She pulled my hair back from my face.

'There, there,' she soothed as another wave of sickness hit me. When it had finished, I slumped back on my pillow and Mary dabbed at my mouth with her handkerchief. 'You *are* in a bad way, aren't you?' she said gently.

Suddenly I could not be angry with her any more. I flung myself in her arms and sobbed and sobbed. My heart was squeezed so tight it felt like a hard lump in my chest. I thought of my childhood: full of pretty dresses and cold-hearted governesses. Never a smile or a word of warmth from Mother, never an embrace or a word of encouragement from Father. I thought of the sameness of all the bleak, grey days, marching one after the other. Then I thought of Jacob and how he let me know love for the first time, and how he had filled my heart before he smashed it into a thousand pieces. And I thought of my mother, my real mother. A girl with dancing green eyes.

'Mary,' I cried, hugging her tight to me. 'It is all so bad. It is the worst thing you can imagine!'

'What is, Miss Ellen? You tell your Mary now. What is so bad?'

'I . . . I am going insane, Mary. I . . . I am sure of it.'

'Don't be so daft, my girl. Whatever makes you say that?'

I loosened my embrace and looked into her face. 'My monthly bleed has not arrived. What am I to do? It is the first symptom of insanity, is it not? Father has always told me so.'

117

The corners of Mary's mouth twitched. 'Well now,' she said. 'I can't say I always agree with your father's opinions . . .'

'If not that,' I said quickly. I had to get rid of the knowledge that had been tormenting me all night. 'If I am not going insane, then I must be with child.'

Mary stiffened for a moment, then began to rock me in her arms. 'Oh, Lord above,' she whispered. 'Oh, my love. It's what I feared. But we cannot be certain. Just because the blood hasn't come yet, it doesn't mean the worst. You haven't been yourself. That can change things and make your bleeds late. I am sure that is what has happened. I am sure of it.'

I pulled away again. 'But . . . but what about Father? He will know something is wrong if you do not take any soiled cloths for him to inspect.'

'Yes,' said Mary thoughtfully. 'But don't you worry about that.'

'But he needs to see proof of my bleeds, Mary. You know he does. And I cannot give him any this time!'

She smiled at me. 'I know,' she said. 'But it just so happens that Ninny has a fresh cut of pig in the kitchen. And blood is blood, is it not?'

25

Queenie

Back at Wild Street Queenie hid her parcels in the scullery cupboard. It was damp and full of greasy cobwebs, but at least no one else would look in there. Mrs Ellis was banging around in the kitchen. She looked up when Queenie came in. 'Had a good afternoon?' she asked.

'Yes, thank you, ma'am.'

'See your family, did you?'

'Yes, ma'am. Had a cup of tea with me mam.' Queenie didn't know why she lied. It had just come out before she thought about it. But she was glad she had. She didn't want to share her afternoon with Mrs Ellis. She certainly didn't want to show off her precious things.

'Well, I'm glad someone had a restful time. Been run off my feet, I have. Not even had time for supper. I'm worn to the bone.' Mrs Ellis made a show of filling the babies' bottles, lifting the jug as though it was a heavy brick. She sighed and wiped the back of her hand across her forehead.

'I'll finish the feeds, ma'am,' said Queenie. 'And bring you some supper too?'

'Yes, yes,' said Mrs Ellis.

'And Mrs Waters. Will she want supper too?' asked Queenie.

'Mrs Waters is out,' said Mrs Ellis in a flat voice. 'She won't be back till late.' She took off her apron and threw it over the back of a chair. 'I'll be in my room.'

'Yes, ma'am,' said Queenie as Mrs Ellis hurried out of the door.

The kitchen filled with silence. Not a soft, hushed comfortable silence. It was hard and brittle. Queenie was afraid to break it. The babies were as still as usual and there was not even a tap dripping. She picked up the jug. Its bottom scraped across the table. Then she began to fill the bottles Mrs Ellis had left. The milk trickled and gurgled and Queenie began to hum. The silence softened and Queenie felt better. She took the full bottles over to the sofa and placed one by the side of every baby. She jiggled the long teats between the babies' lips and shook them all gently. One or two stirred and tried to suck at the rubber in their mouths. They were so tired they barely managed to swallow a drop. Little Rose was fast asleep. Queenie tickled her feet, but could not get her to open her eyes.

'I was going to show you my treasures,' Queenie whispered to her. 'You'll have to wait till morning now.'

Queenie set out cold meat and bread on a tray and carried it up to Mrs Ellis's room.

'Come!' instructed Mrs Ellis when Queenie tapped on her door. She was sitting in her chair with her feet up on a velvet stool. She had a glass of brandy in her hand and the orange flames of the fire were reflected in the golden liquid. She nodded to Queenie to place the tray on the table beside her. 'That will be all,' she said.

'G'night, ma'am,' said Queenie. She thought it was

strange how sad Mrs Ellis looked, sitting in her comfy chair by a warm fire. Queenie thought that one day, when she had all that, pretty ornaments, lace curtains, thick rugs and a house to put it all in, she would be the happiest person alive.

Back downstairs, Queenie fetched her parcels from the scullery cupboard. She put them carefully on the kitchen table and sat down. She picked up the brown paper package first, and put it to her nose. The smell of sweet roses seeped through the paper. She undid the string slowly, savouring the moment. The paper crackled as she unfolded it from around the soap. She ran her fingers over the waxy surface, and sniffed them. Now she smelt of roses too. Next, she turned to the silver tissue package. It was so soft and delicate. It rustled like silk skirts when she unfolded it; carefully so it didn't tear. She picked up the ribbon and let it fall to its full length. It felt like water running through her fingers. She would wear it on her next afternoon off, she decided. She would wash her hair first, in the rose-scented soap. Then she would tie the ribbon in a big bow and it would shine like gold against the blackness of her hair. She wrapped up her treasures carefully and hid them back in the cupboard.

Before she settled on her mattress, Queenie checked on the babies. It was usual to leave them with their bottles during the night in case they woke to feed. She felt their napkins, hoping that Mrs Ellis had done it earlier. They were all of them dry except for Little Rose. She was sopping wet and smelt sour. Queenie sighed. It was the last thing she felt like doing. She pulled off Rose's pink blanket and unpinned her napkin. Something didn't feel right. The baby's legs were cold and rigid. Queenie pulled back. She straight away knew that Rose was gone. She didn't know how to feel for a moment. Babies come and go all the time, she told herself. She thought of the baby at home and how she'd been glad it had died. She wasn't sure she was glad that Rose was dead, though. But she was dead. Queenie felt her little chest. She was definitely gone. And that was that.

Mrs Ellis was very efficient. Queenie thought she'd be mad as a wet hen. Blame her for not looking after Rose properly. But she wasn't. 'Never mind,' she said. 'Another one gone to Jesus. Best place for her.' She took Rose away and told Queenie to get to bed. It was hard to sleep, though. And although Queenie knew Rose was best off out of it, she couldn't rid herself of the picture she'd had in her head of Rose being fetched by a finely dressed lady and being taken away to a healthy place in the country.

26

Ellen

A week went by, and then another. Still the blood did not arrive. Mary asked me the same question every morning. 'Has it come yet, miss?' Every morning I shook my head. It got so that she did not bother to ask the question any more. She needed only to look at my face to see the answer.

My life on the surface went back to how it was before Jacob. I worked on my sewing and I attended to Mother on the rare occasions she asked for me. I took to walking in the garden again. The air soothed me and relieved the sickness that took hold of me every morning. I took my meals with Mother and Father, although I could hardly stomach Ninny's cooking any longer, and I was polite to Father's colleagues who sometimes joined us in the evening.

Everything was just as it had been all my life. Except now I had the biggest and most awful secret to conceal.

Mary tried to reassure me. 'All will be well. You'll see.' But I knew all would not be well. However many times Mary told me my bleeds would return soon, I knew she was wrong. The blood would not come, because I was with child. I knew it to be true. I felt different; changed. I imagined Jacob's offspring growing inside me, squirming and sucking away at my strength. It was a monster planted there against my will, and I was afraid. More afraid than I had ever been.

I hid away in the library most days, searching through Father's books for mention of any maladies which might be mistaken for my condition. I could find none. I was always careful to replace the books in the exact place from where I had taken them.

I could not lose myself in my own books any longer. Romances and mysteries did not engage my attention. I began to flick through Father's copy of *The Times;* distracting myself by reading the theatre listings, reports concerning the engagements of the royal family and the strange case of a Welsh girl who fasted to death. I bypassed the Parliamentary pages; that business bored me. But the court pages engaged my imagination and I spent hours reading of the trials of thieves, murderers and swindlers.

One day, I happened upon a court report at the bottom right-hand side of the page which caused the hairs on my arms to stiffen. I read it again and again.

The Times

April 6, 1870

LAMBETH. Mr. Charles Smith, and Mr. George Thomas – the former being a surgeon, and the latter a chemist – were placed at the bar before the Hon. G.C. BARTON, on a remand for being concerned in using a certain instrument, with the view of procuring abortion, on the person of a young woman at Clapham.

The first witness called was Miss Eliza White. In the

month of October last, she stated, an improper intimacy took place between herself and a Rev. George Campbell, who lodged at her mother's house. 'In the month of December I had some conversation with Mr. Campbell as to the state of my health. As a consequence of this conversation I visited the shop of the prisoner Thomas. I accompanied him into the surgery behind the shop where he felt my bosom and my stomach and told me I was in the family way. He said that he had got a friend who would put me all right. He said I would have to pay 10 shillings. On the following Monday, I saw the prisoner Thomas again at the chemist's shop in Leather Lane. He told me he had seen Dr. Smith and 'he would do the job for the 10 shillings'. He gave me a bit of paper with Dr. Smith's address upon it. I went to Dr. Smith's address, and asked for him. I was directed into the surgery. Dr. Smith pulled down the blind, and was going to examine me, but he would not do it without the money down. I gave him the 10 shillings and he told me to lie on my left side on a sofa in the room, and I did so. He used some instrument under my clothes. A full quarter of an hour elapsed during the operation. I cannot tell how far the instrument went, but during the operation, in which both the prisoner's hands were engaged, I felt something going round like a worm or a corkscrew. There was not any particular pain. I went every day for about a week and on each occasion that I went the operation was the same. I lay on my side every time and felt a pain, a short pain, when the instrument was used. Towards the end of the week he brought me some powders, which were taken in water, and were very nasty to the palate. They were of greyish colour, and gave me great pain in my stomach. I felt very ill indeed. Dr. Smith said, that the 'pains were coming on' and, 'it will be soon over.' My pain at this time was very great, and Dr. Smith took something from me with his hand, which he put into a piece of paper and carried away with him.'

The words of Eliza White went round and round in my head. She had been with child . . . then it had been taken from her. Abortion. I had rarely seen or heard the word before. I had certainly never understood its meaning. I folded the newspaper and took it to my room. I hid it under my mattress so I could read the story again later that night. It was all I could think about. There must be others like Dr Smith, I realised. Plenty of others. But how I would even begin to find someone like that was beyond me.

Mary continued to bring tinctures for me to drink. Cinnamon water to calm my sickness, and raspberry tea, 'a cure for interrupted menstruation', she told me. But for all of her efforts, nothing changed. Another week passed, and then another. Mary sorted out my unused rags and took them to the kitchen. I did not ask what she found to soak them in this time, but Father inspected them as normal and dismissed her without comment. Now I had missed two bleeds. Mary could not deny it any longer. Now we *both* knew what had to be true.

'Oh, what is to be done, miss? What is to be done?' Mary was pacing around my room. 'We cannot hide it for long.

126

And your father! I cannot imagine what he will do!' She threw her hands in the air. 'I wish we could send you away somewhere. My sister would have you. I know she would. You could stay there for a few months to have the baby. Then you could come back and nobody would be any the wiser. But what excuse would we give to where you were? Maybe . . . maybe . . .' She was talking fast, stumbling over her words. 'Maybe we could say my sister is sick. That you had offered to go and nurse her. What do you think, miss? Would your father let you go?'

'Mary, please stop.'

'No, miss. Something has to be done soon. Before you begin to show. We must think what is to be done.' She paused and put her hand to her head. Then she gasped. 'He will dismiss me! He'll know I helped you hide your condition. He'll put me on the streets!'

She looked at me, helpless, waiting for an answer.

I went to my bed and pushed my hand under the mattress. I drew out the copy of *The Times* that was folded back at the court report I now knew word for word. I handed it to Mary and bade her read it. She sat in my armchair and held the paper close to her face. She was proud of knowing her letters, so I patiently waited for her to finish.

Eventually she looked up at me and let the paper fall from her hands and onto the floor. 'What are you thinking of, miss?' she whispered, a look of horror on her face. 'You surely can't be thinking of doing something so . . . so *evil*!'

I had not expected Mary to react in such a way. I had thought she would be pleased that I had found a possible solution. 'But . . . but,' I stuttered. 'Don't you see, Mary?

It is the answer! All we need do is find a doctor willing to help!'

'One who will kill you in the process, no doubt! As well as the child!'

I had never seen Mary as angry.

'You mustn't think of this any more, miss. Put it out of your mind.'

'But Mary, it is the only choice! You must see!' I needed her to agree. I needed her to help me. She was the only one who could find me such a doctor.

'I won't have anything to do with such an idea,' she stated. 'To kill an unborn child is the most evil of crimes. Many have hung for less. Do you know how many young girls have died alone in back rooms? How many have bled to death, their unborn children ripped from their wombs? I'll have nothing to do with it, I tell you!' She stood and looked at me; her eyes hard and her chin quivering with indignation.

The belief that had grown inside me the last few days, the belief that I had found the answer and that all would be well, was shattered. The familiar weight of black hope-lessness returned.

'What am I to do, then, Mary?' I sobbed. 'What am I to do?'

Mary's face softened and she came to put her arms around me. 'I will write to my sister,' she said. 'She will agree to have you there, I know she will. We just need to be able to persuade your father to spare you.'

'If . . . if I go to your sister, what will happen to the child when it comes?'

128

'She would find it a home, miss. My sister would make sure it was well looked after. Don't you worry about that.'

'I am not worried about it being looked after,' I said. 'I just want it to disappear.' For the first time I understood how my real mother must have felt. How she had had no choice but to leave me behind. She would have been glad to get rid of me, I knew. I almost laughed to think how I had so unknowingly followed in her footsteps.

I put my hand on my stomach. I felt a roundness, a soft swelling that only I knew was there. The child was so tiny; hardly there at all yet. But already it had ruined my life.

I was shocked and frightened by the power it had over me and my body.

27

Queenie

Mrs Ellis had taken to spending most of her days with Queenie. She came down to the kitchen early each morning and sat drinking her tea while Queenie stoked the fire, fetched in more coal and swept the floors. She helped Queenie wash the babies and made sure their bottles were topped up with *the Quietness*. Queenie decided she didn't mind having her there. It was good to have someone to talk to. When the morning jobs were done, she asked Queenie to come and sit with her out in the backyard. It was summer now and the kitchen was stuffy and airless. It was a relief to sit out for a while.

Mrs Ellis told Queenie about her husband Thomas and how he had caught typhus and died half insane in a lunatic asylum. 'Terrible it was. I do so miss him.'

Queenie told her about Mam and Da and the little ones. About selling apples and pears on the streets and how the baby had died. When Mrs Waters came out looking for them, Mrs Ellis jumped up. Her voice changed and she told Queenie to do things that had already been done. Mrs Ellis was scared of her sister. Queenie could tell.

There were no more ladies in the house. The last lady's baby had come early and never taken a breath. The doctor was called out for that one. The lady had insisted. Queenie had opened the door and shown him the way to the lady's room. She felt so proud when she said, 'Yes, sir? Can I help you?' and 'Please follow me. I'll show you the way.' Not long after, an undertaker came to take the baby away and the lady had gone by morning.

There were eight babies on the sofa now. One evening when Mrs Ellis had had a drop too much brandy, she told Queenie how Mrs Waters met the mothers at Waterloo Station. They came from all over, she said, with their unwanted infants. Mrs Waters got ten pounds for taking the babies in. Sometimes more if the mother was rich. 'Sshh, though,' Mrs Ellis had giggled. 'Don't let on I told you so.'

Queenie thought hard about the money. If Mrs Waters got ten pounds for every baby, she must be as rich as a duchess. It was the best kind of secret. She could hardly believe it was that easy to earn so much money.

Queenie was used to the babies coming and going. She wasn't surprised when one went or another one appeared. She didn't give any of them names any more. It wasn't worth it. They were never around for long enough. Mrs Ellis trusted her to run all the errands now. She didn't like to go out herself. 'I don't know how I managed before you came along,' she said to Queenie.

There were always fresh bottles of Godfrey's Cordial to be picked up from Mr Epps the chemist. Queenie didn't like to call it *the Quietness*. She made sure to always call it by its proper name. There was milk to fetch and bread and meat, and often a bottle of brandy or two. There were letters to be taken to the post office and replies to be brought back. There were so many; mostly from mothers making enquiries. Mrs Ellis wrote out advertisements to put in the papers and sent Queenie to post these too. Queenie hadn't meant to look, but the envelope wasn't stuck down.

Discreet rooms offered to ladies. All comforts provided, one advertisement said. And another, *Married couple in good circumstances willing to adopt healthy child, nice country home. Terms, £10.*

Queenie puzzled at that one. Maybe it was what Mrs Ellis used to put when her husband was alive. Still, it was a good lot of money the sisters were getting. She wished Da could know how his big gal had landed on her feet. He'd be so proud of her. I'll go back soon and show 'em all how well I've done, Queenie promised herself.

The next time Mrs Ellis sent Queenie out on errands, she had to walk further than usual to fetch a new lot of Godfrey's Cordial.

'Best you go to the chemist on Duke Street. Leave Mr Epps alone for a while. Don't want him wondering why we get through so much of the stuff, do we?' Mrs Ellis said with a pleasant smile.

'He never asks,' said Queenie. 'But if he does I'll just tell 'im we have lots of fretful babies!'

'Oh no,' said Mrs Ellis. The smile left her face and she clutched her shawl around her throat. 'Don't ever do that. You know Mrs Waters don't like anyone to know her business. No . . . you run along to Duke Street now.'

Queenie was glad of the walk. The new chemist hadn't asked any questions and now she had the new bottle of Godfrey's Cordial tucked safely in her pocket. She took her time coming back. The sun slipped warmly over her bare arms. She felt hugged and safe. Her mouth was dry, though, and she had a sudden yearning for an orange. She hadn't had one for the longest time, but she remembered how the flesh burst in her mouth and how sweet the juice tasted.

A way down the road across the other side she could see a grocer's on the corner. The greens of cabbages, the reds of apples, the milky whites of turnips and the yellows of melons shimmered in the distance. She quickened her pace, already tasting the orange in her mouth. As Queenie got to the corner, a newspaper boy took up his position, his arms piled with papers.

'DEAD BABIES DUMPED ON THE STREETS!' he yelled. 'READ ALL ABOUT IT! ANOTHER BODY FOUND WRAPPED IN BROWN PAPER! READ ALL ABOUT IT!'

A tingle ran through Queenie's body and seemed to pull at the roots of her hair. She carried on walking, feeling breathless and hot. She didn't want to have heard those words. She walked fast, knowing that the faster she walked, the quicker the words would disappear. She began to run, not stopping until she got to Wild Street. Only when she was safely inside did she let the memory of Mrs Waters carrying the brown paper package out of the scullery slip into her head. It shook her up to think about it. She tried to push the thought away; to hide it behind the curtain in her head. Why was the world shouting about what she was trying so hard not to think about? It was none of their business. They had no right to pry. Just when everything was going so well.

28

Ellen

It came as no surprise that Father refused Mary's request that I nurse her sister. I had known it was clutching at straws. There was nothing left to do now but wait and hope for a miracle.

The weeks passed and my gowns grew tighter. Mary did her best to lace me in as tight as she could. I took to wearing my shawl at all times. I wore it hanging loose over my bosom so it helped disguise my growing figure. I knew I looked well. My skin glowed and my hair grew thick and glossy. I could sense Father watching me closely at the dinner table. I kept my head down and did not catch his eye. I made sure I was seated before he came in to dine and when I left the table I turned myself in such a way that my back was always to him.

Safe in my room in the evenings, Mary loosened my corset so I could breathe freely. The relief was only momentary. Most nights I could not wait for the mornings to arrive so I could be safely laced up again, despite how uncomfortable it had become.

One morning as I lay in bed watching Mary sort my corset and gown for the day, I felt a strange sensation; like wings fluttering about my insides. It stopped for a moment and I held my breath. Then it came again; a fragile butterfly trapped in my belly. 'Mary,' I whispered. 'There is something wrong. I have a peculiar feeling inside me.'

She turned to me. 'Does it hurt, miss?'

'Oh no,' I said. 'Not at all. But it is very odd. Like a . . . like a tapping.'

Mary smiled and came to put her hand on my stomach. 'It's the quickening, miss. It's your baby's first stirrings.'

I looked at her, but could not speak. I lay still, not daring to move. Then I felt it again; a tap, tap, tapping inside me. The child was alive and wriggling. It was letting me know it was there. A surge of dread filled me up.

'Oh, Mary,' I said. 'It is truly happening.'

'Yes,' she said with a sigh. 'I fear this child is coming, whether we want it to or not.'

It was late. I had read until my eyes were heavy. I blew out my candle, settled into my pillow and waited for sleep to come. The child was still now. There were no more flutterings. I imagined it lying in wait inside me, waiting for me to sleep, so it could prod me awake again.

There was a noise. I opened my eyes. The door creaked and I saw a shadow and the flicker of a candle. 'Mary?' I whispered. What did she want at this late hour?

The candle moved into my room and I saw at once that it was not Mary. Father's bulk filled the doorway and the smell of cigar smoke stung my nostrils. My heart was racing, the thumping filled my head. What did he want? He had never come to my room before. I pulled my covers up to my chin and slid further down the bed. He walked over to me and shone the candle in my face.

'I see you are awake already,' he said. 'That will save me the trouble.' He took hold of my sheets and flung them off me. 'Get up and get dressed,' he ordered.

'What . . . what is happening, Father? Is something wrong? Is Mother ill?' I looked around frantically for my shawl. I could not have Father see me in my nightgown. I had to hide my condition.

'Hurry, girl. What are you waiting for?'

'I just need my shawl, Father.' I could not see well enough in the light of his candle. But I dared not light another one.

'You do not need your shawl! Do you think I am such an idiot? Such a fool that I have not known about your condition since almost the very beginning?'

What was he saying? That he knew about the child?

'Get up!' he hissed. 'Get up now!' I was shivering with fear, my legs trembling. I climbed from my bed and stood, not knowing what to do next. Father stared at me. His eyes travelled up and down and rested on the shape of my pregnant belly, shrouded in my nightgown.

'Look at you, you little whore. I should have known you would never amount to anything. Education and manners have been wasted upon you. Now get your gown on!'

'But why, Father? Why must I get dressed?' I wanted to crawl back into bed, to bury myself deep under the covers and to sleep. I wanted to pretend this was not happening, that it was all just a nightmare.

'Did you actually think you could hide from me? Deceive me with pig's blood? Hide your sins under a well-placed shawl?'

'But Father, it was not my fault. You must believe me! I am innocent. It was Jacob, Father. He . . . he forced himself on me.'

'Do not utter that boy's name to me!' Father hissed. 'And do not use the weakness of men as an excuse for your lack of morality! I will wait outside your door while you dress. Now hurry!'

'But Father, please!'

He turned away from me to walk from the room. Fear was thudding through me. Did he mean to throw me out on the streets? Could he be so cruel?

'Father . . .' The word caught in my throat as tears streamed down my face. 'I know about my real mother,' I managed to say. He stopped and turned back to look at me. 'I know about Dolly,' I said. 'You kept me then. Please don't throw me out now.'

Father walked towards me. His face tightened and he narrowed his eyes. 'It is all arranged.' He touched his candle to another beside my bed. The flame caught and quivered. Father took hold of my chin and stared into my eyes. 'It is true,' he said thoughtfully. 'The sins of the mother are revisited in the child.' He dropped his hand. 'You have two minutes. And you may wish to pack a bag.' He left the room, the door banging shut behind him.

I do not know how I dressed. My hands were trembling, my teeth were chattering. I could not reach to do all my buttons. I pulled a carpet bag from a cupboard and found some underclothes and another gown to put in it. 'Mary,' I sobbed quietly. 'Mary, please come to me.' I knew she would not. She would be asleep at the top of the house. When she came to wake me in the morning she would find my bed empty. Then a terrible thought occurred to me. Had Father thrown her out too? He must know how she tried to help me. Had he made her pack her bags? I cried harder, thinking I might never see her again.

The door opened and Father came in.

'It is time to go,' he said. 'Pick up your bag.'

I could not speak. My voice felt like a lump of coal lodged in my throat. Father took me by the arm, and by the light of his candle he led me down the stairs. I was numb. I could not think. Father took me out of the front door and down the steps. There was a carriage waiting at the bottom. I could hear the soft breath of the horses. Father spoke to the driver in low murmurs, then took something out of his pocket and handed it to him. The driver nodded his head and touched his hat. Then Father opened the carriage door and gestured for me to climb inside. He pushed my bag in after me and, without another word, he closed the door.

It was dark and stuffy inside; the curtains were closed. There was a jolt and I was thrown back in a seat as the horses began to move. 'No,' I whispered. Then louder. 'No!' I pushed the curtains to one side and banged on the window. 'No!' I shouted. 'Father! Mary!'

I saw the dark outline of Father walking back up the steps to the front door. He did not turn around. I looked up at the house and I saw a light flickering in the topmost window.

'Mary! Mary!'

Then it was gone. The house disappeared, the street disappeared and the horses kept pulling.

29

Queenie

It was hot in the kitchen. Queenie was breathless and agitated after her fast walk back from the chemist shop. Her skin was sticky and uncomfortable. Mrs Ellis was asleep in the kitchen chair, an empty glass on the table beside her. The newspaper boy's words echoed around Queenie's head. *Dead babies dumped on the streets.* Queenie checked on the babies. Eight of them sleeping peacefully, a bottle of milk resting by each head.

Queenie walked quietly into the scullery. It was cooler in there, with no fire. She splashed her face and the back of her neck with water. Still the boy's words banged in her head. *Another body found wrapped in brown paper.* There was no room for any other thoughts. No matter how hard she tried. Just the same words repeating themselves over and over. She scooped up a handful of water and drank it. Drops dribbled down her chin and splashed back into the bowl. She needed to do something to make it all all right. She knew what she had to look for.

She began to search the cupboards, bringing out piles of old rags, brushes and empty glass bottles. She pulled storage jars, an old rolling pin, a bag of laundry bluing and an enamel jug from off the shelf. Queenie looked inside the jug and her belly tightened when she saw a small roll of brown paper. She turned the jug upside down, and the paper and a coil of string fell out onto the floor. Queenie stared and stared, her heart thumping loudly in her ears. She had no idea what to do. Then without knowing quite how it happened, she found herself picking up the paper and string and shoving it outside with the kitchen rubbish.

There, now she didn't have to think about it any more. Her heart slowed and began to beat at its proper pace. She took a deep breath and put everything else back in its place.

'Queenie? Is that you?' Mrs Ellis shouted through from the kitchen.

'Yes, ma'am. Just coming,' Queenie shouted back. She fastened her apron around herself and picked up the new bottle of Godfrey's Cordial to take to Mrs Ellis.

Later that evening Queenie took her candle over to the babies. She looked at them one by one. They were the lucky ones, she thought. They were here in the warm, with milk to drink and a place to sleep. Better than being out on the streets with a starving mother and no hope. She thought of the miserable room at home, and the cold and the hunger. Even Mam and Da hadn't been able to keep the last baby alive. She lay on her mattress and hugged herself tight. Only then did she realise she'd forgotten to buy the orange. Tomorrow, she thought. I'll get one tomorrow. Then she blew her candle out and the darkness closed in.

Queenie dreamt of Da. He was sauntering down the street with a tray of oranges around his neck. The oranges were piled high into a tower, each orange as big as a baby's head. Da was singing and a crowd gathered around him to listen. The crowd grew bigger. It pressed in on Da, who grew smaller and smaller. The oranges began to spill from his tray. They rolled on the ground and disappeared between the legs of the crowd. Da cried out. He bent down and tried to catch the oranges but they rolled away too quickly. There was only one orange left in the tray. Da held it tenderly in his hands As the crowd walked away, Da wrapped the orange safely in a piece of brown paper.

30

Ellen

The carriage lurched through the night. I felt as though I was melting away. Like a burning candle, drip, drip, dripping into nothingness. My mind was a blank, the future was a blank. I was terrified.

It seemed to take a long while before the horses began to slow. We came to a halt and all was still for a while. Then a woman's voice, harsh and rough, said, 'We'll take over from here, thank you.' The carriage door opened and a face peered in. It was a tired, faded face framed by a mess of bright orange hair.

'Good evening, Miss Swift,' she said, holding her hand out to me. 'May I help you down?'

I shrank away from her. 'Who . . . who are you?' I whispered.

'I'm Mrs Waters. Now come on. Let's get you in the house and make you comfortable.'

'But I do not know you! Why am I here?' My voice rose to a wail. Panic gripped me. I wanted to scream.

'Calm down, Miss Swift. Don't make a fuss now. We don't want the neighbours woken, do we?'

'But I want to go home,' I sobbed.

'I'm sure you do,' said the woman. 'But you will be

staying here until your child is born. Your father has arranged it all.'

'No!' I screamed. 'I want Mary! I do not want to stay with you!'

'Sshh! Now come on! The carriage isn't going anywhere with you still inside. And I'm sure you don't wish to spend the night in there.' She held her hand out to me again. There was something about her that repulsed me, something about her fat, red fingers.

'No,' my voice shook. 'No, I do not want to come!'

'You have no choice, I'm afraid,' she said. She grabbed my arm and began to pull at me. 'Come on, now. Stop fussing. We'll make you a nice pot of tea when we get inside.'

She pulled harder and jerked me towards the carriage steps. I felt my body slump and grow loose. I was so tired. I allowed her to pull me the rest of the way out.

I was standing on a pavement, facing a dirty, gloomy-looking house. In the grey light of the night, the front door looked like a dark gaping mouth. Hot tears filled my eyes and I could not stop the great gulping sobs that spilled from my mouth.

31

Queenie

There was a loud banging and the sound of sobbing. Someone shook Queenie's shoulder. She opened her eyes and saw Mrs Ellis standing over her.

'Ah, good. Wake up now. We need your help for a minute. Put the kettle on and make some tea, will you.'

Queenie blinked her eyes awake. 'Yes, ma'am,' she mumbled.

Mrs Ellis left the kitchen. Queenie lit a candle then pulled her dress over her head. She sleepily poked at the fire to wake it up too. The sobbing noises grew louder before slowly fading into the distance. Queenie wasn't sure if they were real or had been part of her dream. The kettle whistled and Queenie filled the teapot. Mrs Ellis rushed back into the kitchen. She was all in a dither, her hand flapping around her head and the flame of her candle dancing around madly.

'Is it ready? Is it ready?'

'Yes,' said Queenie, nodding towards the table. 'The pot is nice and hot.'

'Good,' said Mrs Ellis. 'Take the tray and follow me.'

They walked through the dark hallway and up two flights of stairs. The sobbing started again and it grew louder when Mrs Ellis opened the door to the top bedroom. She beckoned Queenie inside. A girl with the whitest face Queenie had ever seen was sitting in a chair with a bulging carpet bag by her feet. She had dark hair that fell over her shoulders in a tangle. Her gown was creased and only half fastened. The silk fabric fell over her swollen belly and pooled in her lap. She was sobbing loudly and shuddering. She seemed surprised by the noises she was making and was trying to gulp down the sobs.

Queenie put the tray down. She wanted to catch the girl's eye and smile at her. But the girl was looking everywhere frantically, not resting her eyes for a second. Mrs Waters turned from straightening out the bed.

'Ah, Queenie. Thank you. Perhaps you could take Miss Swift's jug and fill it so she can wash herself?'

It looked to Queenie that washing herself was the last thing on the girl's mind.

Mrs Ellis came with her back to the kitchen. 'She's very young, ma'am,' ventured Queenie. 'Don't look no older than me.'

'If she's old enough to be with child, she's old enough to have done the tempting,' sniffed Mrs Ellis.

'She looks fair frightened, ma'am,' said Queenie as she filled the jug with water.

'And as well she might. But don't forget how fortunate she is. Plenty of girls in her state will be birthing on the streets. Now, here, I'll take the jug back up. She'll be settled by morning, I'm sure. You can take her breakfast to her,' she said as she sailed out of the room.

Queenie felt wide awake then. There was still hot water in the kettle, so she made a cup of tea and sat in Mrs Ellis's chair by the fire. It was so warm and peaceful. Queenie felt safe wrapped in the darkness with only the glow of the flames to light up her space. It was all quiet and she thought of the girl in the bedroom at the top. She wondered if she had taken herself to bed yet. Mrs Ellis was right. She was one of the lucky ones, that girl. It was all taken care of for her. She would have all the comforts. And when her baby came she could leave it behind and go back to her life like nothing had ever happened. There was no need for her to be sobbing.

32

Ellen

I woke suddenly. My eyes were tight and aching. There was a pain in my head, pressing down across my brow. I wondered why Mary had not come to wake me. I opened my eyes slowly. A chink of daylight knifed through the room from between a gap in the curtains. I winced and blinked hard. I saw ivory curtains with faded roses climbing across the surface. The hems had come unstitched in parts and dragged across the floor. I suddenly remembered where I was.

I closed my eyes again and pushed my face into the pillow. It did not smell right. Instead of clean cotton and lavender, I smelt dampness and the woody scent of a morning chamber pot. I rolled over and pushed the covers off me. The mound of my belly seemed to have grown larger. The child jabbed at my insides; little punches to let me know it was awake. The night came back to me in a blur. Father's cold anger, the breath of horses, the hollow emptiness of a carriage and a strange woman with bright orange hair. I needed to know who she was. I needed to know *where* I was.

I climbed out of bed and drew back the curtains. Dust flew into the room. The sunlight picked it up and sent it swirling through the air. I coughed. I looked around and saw a grey film settled on everything: the scuffed floorboards, two small tables and on the back and arms of a threadbare chair. Green striped paper was peeling from the wall above the bed and black patches of damp darkened the corners of the room. There was a fireplace across from the bed and a small bookcase. Above the fireplace was an ornate gilt mirror with empty candle holders.

I looked at the girl in the reflection and I did not recognise her. The girl in the mirror was deathly pale. Dark circles were scoured under her eyes. Her lips were shrivelled and dry and her dark hair hung in lifeless knots.

I turned away and went to look out of the window. I saw immediately that I was at the back of a house. But there were no lawns to gaze at or colourful flowerbeds to please the eye. Instead there were rooftops and chimneys and a patchwork of back yards with lines of washing hanging limply in the sun. I had no idea where I could be.

There was a knock at the door. I jumped away from the window and rushed back to the bed. The knock came again. I pulled the covers over me. Again the knock came, louder and more persistent.

'Who is it?' I asked. My voice sounded thin and barely there.

'It's Queenie, miss. Got your breakfast here. Can I come in?'

It did not sound like the woman with the orange hair. It was somebody young. Like one of the housemaids at home. 'Yes, yes. Come in,' I said.

I heard the turn of a key and the door opened. A dark-haired girl poked her head around the door.

'You decent then, miss? Oh yes, can see you are. I'll just pop your breakfast down here then, shall I?' She put the tray down without waiting for my answer. 'See you've opened your curtains, miss. Lovely day, ain't it?' She smiled at me and two dimples appeared in her cheeks. She picked up the teapot and began to pour.

I noticed how strangely she was dressed. Her apron was tied around a blue silk day dress that was trimmed with lace. Her hair was held back with a yellow ribbon, and on her feet she wore a pair of old, worn boots that looked far too big for her feet.

'Here you go, miss.' She handed me a cup.

'Thank you,' I managed to say. 'Your name is . . . Queenie? Is that right?'

'Yes, miss. Named after Her Majesty, I am. You feeling better this morning, miss?'

I had a glimmer of a memory from the terrible night just gone. She had been here, in the room, this Queenie girl. I remembered her eyes. Green and knowing, like the eyes of a cat. My hands shook. I could not keep my cup steady in its saucer. Tea slopped over the sides. Queenie took the cup and saucer from my hands.

'Maybe you'd be best having that in a bit, miss,' she said gently.

I nodded my head and gulped hard. 'Where . . . where am I?' I could not hold my tears back any longer in this strange room with its strange smells and with this strange girl who was not Mary.

'Don't worry, miss,' she said to me. 'You'll be quite safe here. I've got me work to do now. I'll come back and see you later.'

Then she was gone.

33

Queenie

Queenie trotted back down to the kitchen, humming under her breath. She liked the new lady. Well, she was a girl, really. She was different from the others. They hadn't talked to her or looked at her mostly. But this one was softer somehow. She seemed so young and lost. Queenie wanted to know her story.

Mrs Ellis was in good spirits. 'How's our young lady this morning?' she asked when she came in the kitchen with an armful of laundry.

'Very weepy, ma'am,' said Queenie. 'She don't seem to know what's happening to her.'

'They're all like that at first. Scared little rabbits. They soon come to terms, mind.' Mrs Ellis smirked. 'She'll be no different . . . Good drying weather today.' She put the laundry on the kitchen table. Queenie sighed. She'd be hours in the scullery now with that lot.

'Oh, Queenie,' said Mrs Ellis. 'Just a minute.'

'Yes, ma'am?' Queenie gathered the laundry in her arms and turned to Mrs Ellis.

'Have you heard anything while you've been out on your errands?'

Queenie's eyes widened. 'Heard what, ma'am?' she asked very slowly.

'About this awful business with babies? Being found dumped about the streets, they are.'

Queenie pulled the washing close to her and held on to it tight. 'Yes . . . well . . . yes, ma'am, I did hear something.'

'Poor little mites,' said Mrs Ellis. 'Their mams couldn't afford to bury them, I expect. Don't you think?'

'Yes,' said Queenie slowly. 'I reckon so, ma'am.'

'Don't know why anyone should think we want to be reading about such things. Do you?' Mrs Ellis was staring at her.

'No, ma'am,' said Queenie.

Mrs Ellis's face relaxed into a smile. 'Right,' she said. 'Well, hurry now, and get this washing out while the breeze is up.'

Queenie's hands were red raw by the time she'd finished scrubbing the sheets and blouses. She put the sopping pile in the tin bath and carried it out to the yard to mangle. It was hard work and her arms ached. It was good to see the fresh linen flapping about freely in the wind. Queenie wished she could feel as carefree, but Mrs Ellis's words were nagging in her head. Had she just been passing the time of day with innocent gossip, or had Mrs Ellis meant more then that? It muddled Queenie to think about it. She didn't want to think about it. Instead, she pegged the last sheet on the line and stood back to admire her work.

34

Ellen

I was weighed down with misery. It was as if a heavy blanket had wrapped itself around me and I could not escape from it. The door of the bedroom was locked from the outside, and although I pounded on it for a while and shouted out, nobody came. I was trapped in this shabby, dirty room in a house full of strangers. I stared out of the window. The girl, Queenie, was hanging sheets on the line. Her arms were pale and thin as matchsticks, yet she lifted the wet linen with ease. She was smiling as she worked. I thought of home, of Mary and her strong capable arms. I missed her so much.

I heard footsteps outside the door and the lock clicked. The woman with the orange hair came into the room. 'Good morning,' she said. 'I trust you slept well?'

I glared at her. 'Who are you and why am I locked in this room?' I demanded.

The woman bristled. 'As I told you last night, my name is Mrs Waters. We only locked the door for your own safety, until you'd calmed down. See, look – you can have the key yourself now.' She went to the door and wriggled the key out of the lock, then held it out to me.

I snatched it from her.

She cleared her throat. 'I am sorry I had to be firm with you last night,' she said. 'But you do understand I only had your best interests at heart. I hope you will report that back to your father.'

'My father?' I said, startled. 'Is he coming here?'

'Oh no,' she said. 'I should think not. Our young ladies don't usually have visitors. They keep themselves to themselves until their babies come.'

'Is that what this place is?' I asked. 'Somewhere to hide me away?'

Mrs Waters bristled again. 'We prefer to think of our home as a refuge or a retreat. Most ladies in your situation do not wish to be seen out in public. They want discretion and to be able to go back to their lives without any scandal chasing at their heels.'

'So all the ladies go home when the time comes?'

'Oh yes, Miss Swift. Indeed they do. Back to their lives as though nothing had ever happened.'

Relief rushed through me. Maybe Father had not thrown me out after all. 'So . . . so Father arranged all this for me?' I asked.

'He did, Miss Swift. You are fortunate he cares for your reputation. Some would have their daughters on the streets without as much as a backward glance.'

I knew at least that was not true. Father cared only for his own reputation. 'And the babies, Mrs Waters? What becomes of them?'

'That is the whole beauty of it, Miss Swift. We take care of them too. You needn't worry about that. You can wash your hands of the whole sorry business.'

For a moment my heart grew lighter, but as she held my gaze I turned cold. There was no hint of kindness in her eyes. I crossed my hands over my belly and looked back to the window. Queenie was still there and dozens of clean sheets were flapping in the breeze.

35

Queenie

Something made Queenie look up. Miss Swift was standing at her window. Her hands were pressed against the glass and her face looked as white as the newly washed sheets. Queenie raised her hand and waved. Miss Swift didn't wave back. She seemed to be looking far into the distance. Queenie quickly gathered up the peg bag and went back inside.

Mrs Ellis was holding one of the babies. Its mouth was open and its head was lolling against her arm. 'I'm afraid this one's a bit poorly,' she said. 'I'm going to have it with me for the rest of the day and the night. So I can keep an eye on it. Don't want the others catching anything, do we?' She wrapped it tight in a blanket. 'You'll be all right with me, won't you my little one?' she cooed as she took the baby away with her.

Queenie saw its bottle still lying on the sofa. She picked it up and went to chase after Mrs Ellis with it. Before she got to the door Mrs Waters strode in.

'Make up some lunch for Miss Swift, will you. But don't bother with any for me. I shall be going out shortly. And Queenie?'

'Yes, ma'am?' Mrs Waters looked at her closely.

'Are you happy here?'

'Yes, ma'am. Course, ma'am.'

'You're happy with us and in your work?'

'Oh yes, ma'am.'

'Well, that's good. Because we trust you. You're becoming part of the family now.' Mrs Waters made an odd movement with her mouth. Queenie realised it was a smile. But Mrs Waters didn't have the sort of face to smile.

'Thank you, ma'am,' said Queenie, and she smiled back, knowing it was the right thing to do.

Miss Swift was asleep in her bed when Queenie took her up a bowl of soup. She hadn't touched her breakfast and the bread was hard and dry. Queenie thought how the little ones wouldn't have cared a bit about that. They would have gobbled the bread down with relish, as if it had come fresh from the baker's oven.

Mrs Waters' words kept coming back to Queenie. *We trust you*, she'd said. *You are part of the family now*. Queenie felt proud of herself. But was it all right to have two families, she wondered? Mam, Da and the little ones, and then Mrs Waters, Mrs Ellis and the babies? First one then the other, or could she have both together? She liked that the sisters trusted her. It filled a hole inside her that had been there ever since she'd kissed Tally goodbye. Mam and Da were fading away now. Every time she tried to picture their faces they crumbled like ashes in the grate. She hadn't had a proper family for a long time, she realised. Just people who shared the same space but wished they were somewhere else. At least here at Wild Street everything felt solid and real and she could enjoy the feeling of being alive.

36

Ellen

I spent the afternoon in bed. I had no appetite and no strength for thought. When I woke there was a bowl of soup grown cold on the table, and when I looked out of the window the washing line was empty. I turned to the bag I had so hastily packed. I had no memory of what I had thrown in and little idea how I would manage in the long weeks ahead. I pulled out a nightgown, my hairbrush, some underclothes, ribbons, pieces of jewellery and a heavy dark blue gown. I laid everything out on the bed; it was all that I had. I picked up the gown and buried my face in the folds of fabric. I smelt the faint warm scent of lavender and it made me long again for Mary and the comforts of my own bedroom.

I took up the brush and began to comb the tangles from my hair. The rhythm calmed me and I brushed for a long time until each lock felt smooth and ordered. Then I stripped naked and washed in the water that had been brought to me the night before. I wiped my feet and legs, then under my arms and over my breasts. My body was so changed. I wiped gently and felt its heaviness. My nipples had grown dark and pale blue veins criss-crossed the swell of my breasts. I squeezed water over my belly and the child inside me shifted, as if startled by the cold. It shocked me to see how big I had grown. My skin was stretched and tight and I wondered how much bigger I would get before I burst open. It did not seem possible that a full-grown baby could fit inside me. I shivered from the cold and from the fear of being so alone. My belly shifted again. 'Be still!' I said out loud. I did not know whether I was talking to the baby or to myself.

37

Queenie

Queenie took extra care with Miss Swift's morning tray. She cut the crusts off the bread and arranged the slices neatly on a plate, and she went out in the yard and picked a small sprig of daisies to put in a glass of water. The young lady was awake and dressed when Queenie went up. She was sitting in the chair with her hands clasped in her lap. She looked as though she'd been waiting for the door to open. Queenie put the tray down and smiled.

'Shall I pour for you, miss?'

Miss Swift nodded and said, 'I . . . I wonder if you would help me with my gown?'

She stood and turned her back to Queenie. The gown was gaping; only half the buttons had been fastened. Queenie started at the top and began to pull the loops over the tiny pearl buttons. The first few fastened easily, but further down Queenie's fingers fumbled to stretch the fabric to meet.

'I'm sorry, ma'am,' she said. 'But these lot just won't do up. You'll be needing a bigger gown, I think.'

The young lady sat down heavily in her chair and sighed.

Queenie poured the tea and then watched how she took delicate sips from the edge of the cup.

Miss Swift picked up a piece of bread, then hesitated for a moment.

'Queenie,' she said. 'Can you please tell me where I am? Where is this house? Am I still in London?'

Queenie laughed. 'Still in London? 'Course, miss! Where else would we be?'

The young lady's cheeks flamed red and she bent her head. 'I . . . I was quite distressed on my journey here. I lost track of time and could not tell for how long I was in the carriage.'

Queenie wished she hadn't laughed. 'Sorry, miss. We're in Wild Street,' she said in a softer tone. 'Not far from Drury Lane.'

'Drury Lane?' the young lady whispered to herself. 'That is not too far from the British Museum and . . . and Gower Street and Euston Square.' She looked up at Queenie. 'It's where my father works,' she said. 'At the University College Hospital. I cannot be too far from home, then.'

Queenie didn't know what to say next. She felt awkward just standing there with nothing to do. Just as the silence between them began to pound in Queenie's ears, Miss Swift turned to her.

'Are you the daughter of Mrs Waters?' she asked Queenie carefully.

'Oh no, miss, no,' said Queenie. 'I just work here is all.'

'So have you seen many like me come and go?'

'One or two, miss. But I ain't been here more than a few months.'

Miss Swift was looking at her as though she needed her to say something more.

'There's nothing to worry about, miss,' said Queenie. 'Mrs Waters and Mrs Ellis will look after you right. And they'll find a good home for your baby when it comes too.' She thought of Little Rose and all the others that were down in the kitchen now. It was best she said nothing about those, she decided. She knew the sisters didn't like their business talked about.

Miss Swift had tears in her eyes now. She reached out her hand to Queenie and held on to her wrist. 'Thank you, Queenie. I needed to hear that.'

Queenie felt so grand to be talking like this with a proper young lady. It seemed the strangest thing. But everything about her new life had been strange at first. This would be no different, she supposed. She was some- body worth talking to now and it felt good. She wasn't just another faceless urchin on the streets any more. She wasn't a grubby, ragged pauper that nobody gave the time of day to. That was her old life, and she was never going back to it.

'Would you have a needle and thread, Queenie, and some scissors?' Miss Swift asked her. 'If you would be kind enough to bring some to me, I could let out my dress.'

'Yes, miss. I'm sure I can find you some.' Queenie picked up the breakfast tray, pulled her shoulders back, and held her head high as she left Miss Swift's bedroom.

The babies were quiet as usual. Sometimes Queenie forgot they were there and was so busy with her chores that she only remembered to check their bottles at the end of the day. Mrs Waters seemed not to notice the babies at all. She was only pleased when they first came into the house. There hadn't been any new ones for a while now, but there was room on the sofa for more. Queenie knew that one day soon, Miss Swift's baby would be at the end of the row, lying there with all the others.

There was no sign of Mrs Waters, Mrs Ellis or the baby that Mrs Ellis had taken away to look after. *It's gone to a new home*, Queenie told herself. She didn't want to think any more about it. She wanted to find a sewing box for Miss Swift. There must be one somewhere in the house, she thought. She wanted to find it to please the young lady; to help her. Miss Swift needed her and that felt wonderful.

Queenie knocked on Mrs Ellis's door. There was no reply. When she knocked on Mrs Waters' door there was no reply either. She turned the handle and found the door was locked. Queenie walked through the house checking each room in turn. The other rooms in the house were unused and mostly empty of furniture. There were only a few strange shapes covered by dust sheets. Queenie threw back the sheets but there was no sewing box to be found, only a moth-eaten velvet sofa, a cabinet full of stuffed birds and a few wooden tables and chairs.

Queenie went back to Mrs Ellis's room and knocked again. There was silence. She tried the handle, expecting the door to be locked like Mrs Waters' had been. But the handle turned and the door opened easily. She shouldn't go in, Queenie knew that. But if she was quick Mrs Ellis would never know.

It was shadowy inside, the curtains were drawn shut and the room smelt of cold ashes. Queenie stood for a moment to let her eyes get used to the gloom. Aside from Mrs Ellis's bed, her chair and velvet stool, a table, a chest of drawers, a wash stand and a wardrobe, Queenie could see nothing that might be a sewing box. She was not surprised. She had never seen the sisters mend a tear or sew on a button.

There were photographs on the mantelpiece over the fireplace. Queenie recognised Mrs Ellis in one of the pictures. She was much younger and was holding a sleeping baby in her arms. Behind her was a dark-haired gentleman all buttoned up in a stiff collar. He had his hand on Mrs Ellis's shoulder and Queenie thought he must be the poor husband who had died of madness. Queenie picked up the photograph. She wondered where the baby was now. All grown up, no doubt. It was strange to think that Mrs Ellis once had a little family all of her own.

Queenie put the photograph back in its place before having one last look about the room. As she turned, her shoulder caught the edge of the photograph frame and knocked it to the floor. It skittered across the wooden floorboards and came to rest by the rug at the side of the bed. Queenie took in a sharp breath. How would she explain to Mrs Ellis if the frame was broken? She hurried across the room and bent to pick the frame up. It was in one piece, there was not a scratch on it. As she went to straighten up, the dark space under the bed caught her eye and she dropped to her knees to get a better look. She saw two boxes, a small wooden one and a larger tin one. Queenie slid them both out and opened the lid of the smaller one. She smiled to herself to see a tangle of threads, ribbons, tapes, tins of needles and a pair of small silver scissors. She took the scissors, a few needles and some thread and put them all in her pocket. Then she pushed the box back under the bed and looked again at the larger one. What harm could it do to look inside that one too? The lid was tight and Queenie had to use her nails to prise it open. She inched it loose, bit by bit. Suddenly the lid sprang open and a musty smell caught in her nostrils. It looked to Queenie like a bundle of blankets had been shoved into the box. She reached inside and pulled at one. Her heart stopped as she saw that the blanket was pink and edged with silk. Queenie pushed her hand further in and pulled out more blankets, some tiny chemises and petticoats, baby flannels and small lace caps. Some of the pieces looked familiar to her. She had washed and dried many of them. What were they doing here when the babies that had worn them had been taken to new homes? Why had their clothing been left behind?

With trembling hands she put everything back inside, hurriedly put the lid back in place and pushed the box under the bed, making sure the rug was straight. She got up from her knees and walked to the fireplace, where she carefully stood the frame back in place, even though her hands were shaking. Her heart was thumping loudly in her chest. Dark thoughts gathered in her head. Babies coming and babies going. And never had she seen or heard the carriages that had been sent to collect them.

She hurried from the room. As the door closed behind her, she hid the picture of the tin box and its contents behind the imaginary sheet that hung inside her head.

38

Ellen

Queenie brought me needles, thread and scissors. I cut fabric from the full skirts of my blue gown and added new panels to my bodice. I sat by the window and looked out over the rooftops as I worked line after line of tiny, neat stitches. The gown fitted me well now and there was room enough for if I grew even bigger in size.

The days passed slowly. I did not leave the bedroom. I grew comfortable there and Queenie brought me everything I needed. She brought fresh water for me to wash every day and cloths for me to dry myself. She took care of my chamber pot and brought my meals to me on a tray. When I developed a longing for stewed apples she brought me a dish with every meal. I read the books in my room and I lost myself in the mysteries of Wilkie Collins's *The Moonstone* for days.

I asked Queenie for some scraps of linen and I spent long hours embroidering delicate flowers and leaves and a large fanciful letter Q. When I gave the results of my labour to Queenie she looked as though she had received a casket of gold instead of the simple handkerchief I had sewn.

She brought me paper and pens and I bade her sit for a while and sketched her, framed by the light from the window.

'That ain't me!' she exclaimed when I showed her the portrait. 'She's somebody pretty.'

'It is you, Queenie,' I assured her. 'And you are very pretty.' I laughed at her as she stared at the picture and touched her face as though she could not put the two together.

'How does your hair sit on your head like that?' she asked me one day.

'Oh, it is easy,' I said. 'Just a few well-placed pins.' I took my brush and combed her hair until it shone. Then I made her sit still while I twisted it into knots and curls and pinned it all into place. I finished the arrangement with a blue satin ribbon and guided her to the mirror so she could see how beautiful she looked. She opened her mouth to speak, but no words came out. She turned her head from side to side and smiled at her reflection. Then she put her arms around me and hugged me tight.

'I look just like a lady,' she breathed. Then we both looked at each other and burst into giggles.

Sometimes I woke in the middle of the night gripped by a terrible fear. I fancied I heard a baby's cry and hurried footsteps disappearing into the distant darkness. For a moment I was certain the child had been ripped from me while I slept. That Father had stolen into my room with his scalpels, and that were I to look down at my body I would see a gaping and bloody hole. Then the child moved inside me and I dared to put my hands on my belly to feel the comfort of warm skin and my own frantic heartbeat.

I often wondered where Jacob had gone. What would he do if he knew his child was growing inside of me? Would he come to me full of sorrow and regret at how he had hurt me? Would he be gentle and loving and want only to look after me and his child? In the sleepless hours of the night I wished hard that this would be true. I fancied I could smell lemons and I remembered the soft touch of his lips and the way my heart had tilted so deliciously. Then I would see his eyes again, as he had looked at me in the garden that last time. In terror, I looked again into the blackness of him and I knew he was empty of feeling. Something important was missing from inside him. Jacob was dangerous. He had taken part of my soul. The boy I had loved had never existed.

39

Queenie

Queenie loved attending to Miss Swift. It made her feel special and important. She loved laying out her tray for breakfast, with the best teapot, teacup and saucer. She loved balancing it all ever so careful as she walked up the stairs, her skirts swishing around her ankles. She always minded to knock on Miss Swift's door and wait for the 'Come in, Queenie!' before she went in.

She would lay the tray on Miss Swift's bedside table, and then open the curtains to let in the morning. When she turned round, Miss Swift would be sitting up in bed rubbing the sleep from her eyes. There was often as not a bemused look on her face, as though she had expected to wake up somewhere else.

It was a Sunday morning. The sisters had left the house early, dressed in their best clothes. Mrs Waters had been twitchy and impatient, barking at Mrs Ellis, 'Hurry, Sarah! Do you want us to be late?' Queenie knew they'd be going to the station to collect another baby. It was always the same way. They'd be in fine spirits when they got back, mind. And with the money they got for the child there was sure to be something extra good for dinner.

Queenie whistled a ditty as she brushed Miss Swift's

gown and shook out her petticoats ready to help her dress.

'What is that tune?' asked Miss Swift. 'I have never heard it before.'

'Oh, you wouldn't have, miss,' laughed Queenie. 'It's one of me da's from the penny gaffs.' She began to sing, '*Oh, me name it is Sam Hall, chimney sweep, chimney sweep, oh, me name it is Sam Hall, chimney sweep. Oh, me name it is Sam Hall, and I robbed both great and small and me neck will pay for all when I die!*'

Miss Swift put her hand to her mouth in shock and whispered between her fingers, 'Queenie!'

'Oh, that's nothing, miss. I know much worse than that! Do you want to hear another?'

'I certainly do not!' said Miss Swift. But Queenie could see that her eyes were smiling.

'I could teach you to whistle,' said Queenie. 'Bet you've never done that before, have you?'

Miss Swift shook her head and took her hand away from her mouth.

'It's easy,' said Queenie. 'Look. Put your lips together like this and just blow.' She let out a long whistle. Miss Swift watched her carefully. Then she pursed her own lips and blew. No sound came out, only a burst of air. Queenie laughed. 'Try again,' she urged. Miss Swift looked serious. She pursed her lips again and this time let out a small breathy whistle. She looked at Queenie in amazement.

'I did it!' she said. 'Did you hear? I did it!' They looked at each other and smiled in delight. Queenie felt warm inside. It was a feeling that was almost as good as the taste of fresh bread on an empty belly.

'What does your father do?' asked Miss Swift as she sipped at her tea.

'He's a costermonger, miss. Sells apples and pears and the like. When he's not drinking, that is.'

'Oh,' said Miss Swift. 'And your mother? What is she like?'

Queenie paused. She thought of Mam and her swollen belly, her strong arms and her worn-out face. She thought of the groans of strange men behind the curtain. She could hardly tell Miss Swift that, could she? 'Mam is just Mam,' she said eventually. 'Pops out babies, mostly!' Queenie's eyes fell to Ellen's belly. 'Oh, sorry, miss,' she said. 'I didn't mean . . .'

Miss Swift shook her head. 'Never mind,' she said. 'Tell me about the rest of your family. It must be so good to have so many of you?'

'Pah!' said Queenie. 'Three little 'uns there were. There'll be four by now. Right pains they are too. Well, maybe Tally's not so bad now he's getting bigger.' Queenie realised she hadn't thought of any of them for an age. Talking to Miss Swift like this brought them all back to mind, when she didn't really want to think about them at all.

Miss Swift looked sad. 'You are very lucky, Queenie,' she said. 'To have a family like that.'

'Me, miss? Lucky?' Queenie was amazed. How could Miss Swift, with all her fancy gowns and pretty jewels and ladylike ways, think that Queenie was lucky?

'Yes, Queenie, you are lucky. You see, you have somewhere you belong.'

For the rest of the day Queenie puzzled over what Miss Swift had said. And for the first time since she'd left home, she imagined what it would be like to go back.

40

Ellen

The weeks turned to months. Summer turned to autumn and I had not once felt the sun on my face. I spent most of my time sitting by the bedroom window. The outside world was contained within the window frame – like a moving painting. I watched the changing skies, and saw leaves turn from a shimmering green to a dull brown before they fell from their branches.

My belly had grown so large. Even though I had let out my gowns as much as possible, they no longer fitted. My nightgown and shawl were the only garments I could wear. But even my nightgown now pulled tight across my belly.

One day, Queenie brought me a length of creamy soft flannel and some tiny chemises. 'For you to make another nightgown, miss,' she said. 'The nights are cold now and you'll be needing something warmer. And these are for the baby when it comes.'

'Oh, Queenie, what would I do without you?' I said. 'You remind me of Mary,' I told her. 'She was the only person I had in the world before you.'

Queenie grinned at me. 'It's no trouble, miss. I like looking after you.' I could tell by the shine in her eyes that she meant every word. I wanted to tell her that her kindnesses meant everything to me now. That I could not have survived it here without her.

I began work straight away on my new flannel night-gown, but the chemises I left to one side. I could not imagine the creature inside me, that squirmed constantly and dug its limbs into my ribs, would soon be wearing the tiny garments.

Queenie often asked about my home. Through her eyes I lived in a palace.

'Do you have a grand piano?' she said. 'And lots of maids? What do you eat, miss? Oh please, tell me about the dinners you have!'

I laughed and told her of Mary and Ninny and the other maids. I told her of the silence around the dining table and of the calf's head Ninny once cooked.

'A whole calf's head!' she exclaimed, as though it was the grandest thing she had ever heard of. She urged me to describe all my gowns and her eyes shone as I told her about my pink silk and my dark blue velvet. She asked about Mother and Father, so I told her of Mother's birds and of Father being a doctor of sorts. 'He cuts bodies open for a living,' I said, hoping to shock her.

'He's a butcher, then?' she said, and I laughed to think how Father would be outraged to hear himself described as such.

'And do you go dancing, miss?' she asked. 'And do the gentlemen queue up for a twirl around the floor?'

I did not answer for a moment. I was wishing my life was as Queenie imagined it to be. I wanted to tell her that it was all true, so that she would not be disappointed in me. But I could not deceive her. That would only be deceiving myself too.

'I do not go anywhere, Queenie,' I said. The sudden deadness in my voice changed the mood between us. 'I did not go anywhere or do anything even before this.' I jabbed my finger at my belly. 'My life was empty.'

'But then . . .' Queenie frowned at me. 'Hope you don't mind me asking, miss. But how did you come to be in your condition?'

I told her then. It was a relief to sit with her holding my hand as I told her the truth. I told her of the loneliness and emptiness of my life and of how Jacob had brought light into the house for the first time. I told her about his dark hair and green eyes, how he'd kissed me and made everything seem wonderful. Then, in a whisper, I told her how he had tricked me and played with me, and with tears choking my voice, I told her of the terrible day in the garden.

'So you see, Queenie, even with my fine house and pretty gowns and jewels, I really have nothing. I have less than nothing. And the worst of it is, I will have to go back there,'

'But you have me, miss,' she said, squeezing my hand tight. 'You'll always have me.'

41

Queenie

It was mid December. Since she'd arrived at Wild Street, Queenie had been putting her wages aside, week by week, in an old tin she'd hidden at the back of the scullery cupboard along with her soap and ribbons. She thought about Mam, Da and the little ones more and more. She wanted them to see how well she'd done for herself, to tell them about Miss Swift and the sisters. She wanted them to see she'd found a good place in the world.

It was Sunday and Queenie had the afternoon off. The sisters were in their rooms snoring in front of the fires that Queenie had laid, Miss Swift was taking her afternoon sleep and the babies were all dosed up as usual.

Queenie took a handful of coins from her tin and hurried to Lowther Arcade. She bought sugar mice for the little ones, a shawl for the new baby and a tin of damp, sweet-smelling tobacco for Da. She would give Mam some rose-scented soap, she decided. They wrapped it up so nice in the shop. For herself she bought a new pair of black leather boots and gave the old ones to a passing urchin. The heels of her new boots clicked when she walked and the laces were long and black as liquorice strings. The little ones would all marvel at her boots, she knew that. None of them had ever had new boots before. Mind you, none of them had ever known Christmas before. It was something that happened for other people. Queenie and the little ones only ever stared in the butcher's window at the fat geese and ducks waiting to be taken to table. They only ever breathed in the delicious smells of baking pies and spiced puddings. They never had a gift or anything to call their own. Queenie couldn't wait to see their faces when they opened her offerings. She was strangely nervous.

It seemed the whole of London was rushing hither and thither as Queenie retraced her steps over Waterloo Bridge. There was an excitement in the air and even the old cab horses seemed to be trotting with an extra skip in their step. Queenie could hardly believe it had been nearly a whole year since she'd left. It had been just as cold back then but she was dressed warmer now, with a thick new shawl, a woollen gown and her new boots polished to a shine.

She turned off the main thoroughfare and walked down the first passageway that led to Mam and Da's court. She had forgotten how bleak and sad it all was. It was as though life stopped short the minute she stepped into the gloom. Faces peered at her from darkened doorways, then disappeared, like rats darting back into their holes. Whispers followed at her back. Then Queenie remembered how odd she must look; done up like a dog's dinner with clean face and new clothes. She was a stranger here now. She clutched her parcel of gifts close to her chest.

Queenie heard Da before she saw him. He was singing,

but there was no trace of the drink in his voice. It was how Queenie remembered it when she was small and Da would sing all the dirty ditties from the penny gaffs to Mam. He would get a clout round the head but would carry on anyway, laughing and saying, 'The smuttier the better I thinks! You likes 'em as much as I do, my gal!'

When Queenie turned the bend in the passage, there he was with his neckerchief back around his throat and him and Tally sitting on the doorstep mending sacks. She hid herself in a doorway to watch them for a while. Tally had grown so big. His arms and legs sprouted out from the ends of his sleeves and trousers. He was laughing at Da's song. Queenie noticed he had his own neckerchief tied around his throat now, green and yellow, the same as Da's.

Then Mam came out the door with a fat baby in her arms. She bent to ruffle Tally's hair and said something in Da's ear. He laughed out loud and smacked her on the behind as she turned to go back indoors. Tally put his sack down and stretched his arms above his head, yawned, then stood up. He looked towards where Queenie was hiding in the shadows. She started to lift her hand to wave, but Tally just blinked, then turned away and went inside. Queenie lowered her hand. Of course he couldn't see her; he wouldn't be expecting to see her. Da gathered up the sacks and stood up too. Queenie wanted to shout out to him, *Da it's me! It's Queenie!* But something stopped her. It was the way they all were together. So happy. Da was in a hurry to get inside. Queenie thought Mam must have boiled the kettle and maybe there was something hot for them all to eat. He didn't even look her way before he went inside too.

A hot rush of shame flushed Queenie's cheeks. She was angry with herself for standing there with an armful of gifts and no one to give them to. They were all getting on well enough without her. Da was there, Mam had a new baby and Tally was all grown up. They didn't need her and her daft trinkets. They didn't need her at all. The thought took Queenie's breath away for a moment. What had she been expecting? That they'd still be missing her after all this time? It had been nearly a year, and not once had she let them know she was safe and doing well. A worm of guilt uncurled in her belly. How could she have done that to them? They most likely thought she was dead. She imagined Tally weeping for her and the thought made her throat tight and her eyes sting. She swallowed hard and rubbed her eyes with the back of her hand. They looked happy enough without her in any case. They'd probably mourned her and forgotten about her by now.

For a moment Queenie felt lost; caught between two worlds. She looked down at her new boots and felt ridiculous and embarrassed. Well, if they didn't need her, thought Queenie, then she didn't need them. She had a new place in the world now and it was far better than this stinking hole. With a last glance at the dark doorway she used to call home, Queenie turned on her heels and hurried out of the tangle of passageways. She trod carefully so as not to muddy the hem of her gown or dirty her new boots too much.

* * *

Queenie heard Ellen's cries of pain sounding through the house as soon as she got back to Wild Street. She threw her parcels on the kitchen table and grabbed the kettle to fill. She would be needed now and she knew exactly what to do.

42

Ellen

I woke with an ache in my back and thought I must have slept awkwardly. Although a small fire was burning in the grate, it was bitter cold in the room and I made my mind up to stay in bed a while. It was hard to move about with my belly so big and the effort to get dressed usually wore me out for the rest of the day. I propped myself up on my pillows and took up my sewing. The room was dim and it tired my eyes to sew by the light of a candle. I must have fallen asleep again and when I woke the fire had gone out. Grey light crept low into the room and I thought it must be late afternoon. My back was aching much worse than before and I was desperate to relieve myself. As I climbed from my bed and reached down for the chamber pot a warm fluid ran down my legs and pooled on the floor. I was surprised and dismayed, as I still felt the need to relieve myself and could not understand what had happened. I was embarrassed that Queenie would know what I had done, but I had no cloths to mop up the mess. Then the first pain came and then the next and I pulled myself back onto the bed.

The pains ripped through me and caught my insides so tight I thought I might die. I bit down hard on my pillow and howled like an animal. I curled into a ball. But still they would not stop. I knelt and held on to the headboard. I hardly knew where I was. Faster and faster the pains came, not giving me a moment to breathe. Just as I thought I could bear it no more, the tightening in my belly loosened and the pains slipped away. I gasped for air and slumped down on the bed. I saw the neat pile of tiny chemises that Queenie had brought. Would a child be dressed in them by the end of the day? Then the pains came again and all thoughts were wrenched from my head.

I was floating on a sea of agony; each wave of pain growing bigger and bigger. I was swallowed up and lost. The real world slipped away from me and time stood still. I called out for Mary but she did not come. The pains kept rolling through me.

Then there was a cold cloth on my brow and hot knives in my belly. And a voice telling me to hush, all would be well. Then I was pushing and pushing and I could not stop and there was a hot rush from inside of me. Then I saw Queenie smiling at me and she was holding a bloodied bundle in her arms.

43

Queenie

Queenie wiped the blood off the baby and wrapped it tight in a soft clean cloth. It looked all there to her, with ten fingers and toes, a tuft of black hair and creamy white skin. It had all happened so quickly, but she was proud she had managed on her own. The worst part had been cutting the cord. It was thicker and tougher than she had imagined. She was worried it would hurt Miss Swift and the baby, as it was part of both of them. But Miss Swift hadn't even noticed. She had fallen into an exhausted trance before the afterbirth had come out. Queenie had wrapped that mess up in old newspaper and thrown it on the fire. It had crackled and spat as it burned.

Miss Swift was stirring now. 'Is it out of me?' she mumbled.

'Here,' said Queenie, tilting the bundle towards her. We've been waiting for you to come round. Do you want to hold it?'

Miss Swift's eyes opened wide. She shook her head hard, a look of alarm on her face.

'Come on,' said Queenie. 'It won't bite!' She pressed the warm little parcel into Miss Swift's arms. Miss Swift stared at Queenie and then down at the baby. She looked to Queenie like a young girl with a doll. Then very gingerly Miss Swift unwrapped the cloth from around the baby.

'Oh,' she said, looking up. 'It is a girl.'

'I know,' said Queenie. 'She's beautiful, ain't she?

'She's perfect,' whispered Miss Swift. The baby was making small bleating sounds and rubbing its face into Miss Swift's chest. 'What is the matter with her?' she asked Queenie. 'Is she quite all right?'

'She's just looking for your ti . . . for you to nurse her,' said Queenie. 'She'll be hungry, that's all. But don't you mind about that. I'll take her downstairs and give her a bottle. Then you can rest some more.'

'I . . . I am not sure,' said Ellen. She looked shyly at Queenie. 'I do not want to let her go yet. I think I would like to feed her myself. Would you . . . would you fetch me a bottle?'

Queenie brought a bottle of milk up from the kitchen. It was the freshest she could find and she had warmed it gently.

'How do I do it?' asked Miss Swift when Queenie handed her the bottle.

'Well . . . you just have to offer her the teat. She'll know just what to do.'

Miss Swift looked at Queenie with wide eyes. 'Is she so clever?' she asked. Miss Swift brought the baby close to and pressed the teat to her lips.

'I'll leave you alone now,' said Queenie. 'You'll be wanting to be private.' She felt strange, like she was intruding on something, that she shouldn't really be there.

188

'No . . . no. Please stay!' said Miss Swift. 'I . . . I need you, Queenie. I could not have gone through this without you. Please don't go.'

Queenie sat on the chair and watched as Miss Swift awkwardly cradled her babe.

'Oh!' said Miss Swift. 'You are right! She is suckling!'

Queenie saw that special look on Miss Swift's face; like she was in the best place in the world. It seemed she had fallen in love with her child in an instant. Queenie remembered Mam looking like that with each new babe; like they were the only reason to keep going. A hole opened up inside her. She missed Mam and the little ones. She missed Da. And she didn't like how much it hurt.

She thought of the babies downstairs. How still and unwanted they were. Would the same thing happen to this baby? Would Miss Swift let her little one be taken to a new home? A picture of blankets and baby clothes stuffed in a tin box flashed through her mind. She saw Mrs Waters coming out of the scullery with a brown paper parcel tucked under her arm, and she heard again the shouts of the newspaper boy. She shook her head hard; pushing the pictures and words back where they had come from. Back behind the imaginary sheet in her head. She could never let anyone know what she had seen.

Footsteps sounded outside the door. Queenie jumped to her feet. The sisters were back and she hadn't done any of her chores or checked on the babies once since she'd come back from her visit home. Mrs Waters walked into the room and took in the scene with one sweeping glance.

'Mrs Ellis needs you downstairs,' she said to Queenie.

Her voice was cold. Queenie didn't want to leave Miss Swift alone but Mrs Waters was already shooing her away and walking towards the bed. Queenie went out into the hallway and as the bedroom door closed behind her, she heard Mrs Waters say, 'Now then. What have we here?'

44

Ellen

'You shouldn't be doing that, Miss Swift,' Mrs Waters said to me. 'I am surprised at you. Only the lower classes nurse their own. Besides, you should be resting.'

'I was only feeding her,' I said. 'She was hungry.'

'Be that as it may, it is not fitting for a lady of your social standing to engage in such an activity. Believe me. Now give the child and the bottle here and I will see it is fed downstairs.'

'But she is asleep now and I do not want to wake her.' The thought of Mrs Waters holding my baby made my stomach churn. She had only been out of me for such a short while. She was so new and untouched. I wanted to study her face, her silky lashes and her lips like tiny plump cushions. I could not let her go. She belonged to me and for the first time in my life I felt the force of real, solid love. 'She is happy as she is, thank you, Mrs Waters,' I said. 'I would like to be alone now so I can rest.'

In truth I was frightened out of my wits to be left alone. My whole body was sore and there was a deal of blood on my sheets. I dared not move for I thought my insides might spill out of me. My little daughter felt so fragile in my arms. I had no idea what to do. Would I know how to be a mother? All I could do for now was to hold her tight.

Mrs Waters set her mouth in a straight line. 'As you wish,' she said.

She swept out of the room and I prayed that Queenie would soon come up to me. I listened to my baby breathing and felt the rise and fall of her chest. She was curled up in the crook of my arm, warm and soft like a ball of newly risen dough from Ninny's kitchen at home. I drifted into a half dream where Ninny was pulling loaves of bread and tins of cakes and pies from the oven. One after the other, until the kitchen table groaned under the weight of them. Then I saw Mother sitting at the end of the table. She was tearing off great chunks of bread and cramming them in her mouth. She was biting into pies and the juices were dribbling down her chin. She was grabbing at handfuls of cake and cream was oozing through her fingers. Her frail frame grew bigger and bigger and her cheeks grew so huge and round they looked fit to burst. Then the heaps of baking turned into a table full of squirming babies and Ninny was pulling more and more from out of the oven. Warm babies freshly baked. I turned to Mother and saw she had a baby in her hands. She was lifting it towards her mouth and I saw her sharp teeth glinting. NO! I shouted. NO!

I opened my eyes. I was trembling and a scream was dying in my throat. I looked down and saw the crook of my arm was empty.

My baby had gone.

I searched around under the sheets and leaned over the side of the bed to check the floor. She was nowhere to be seen. I thought I must still be dreaming. *Wake up!* I told myself. *Wake up!* My head was whirling. *I must find her, I must find her*. I needed to get help now!

I got up from the bed. My legs were barely able to hold me; I was as unsteady as a newborn foal. The room swam in front of my eyes as I took tiny steps towards the door. My stomach felt as if it was falling out of me and blood poured warm and slow down my legs. I grabbed on to the handle to steady myself and for the first time since I had arrived at this house, I left my bedroom.

The landing was dim and dusty. A candle burned on a table in the corner. I picked it up and shuffled my bare feet across the floorboards as I made my way to the top of the stairs. I held on to the banisters to stop myself from swaying and slowly made my way down two flights. At the bottom of the stairs I found myself in a tiled hallway. There were two closed doors, but the muffled voices I could hear seemed to be coming from the other end of the room. I followed the noises and found myself standing at the top of a small dark stairwell. There was a chink of light shining from under the door at the bottom. I walked slowly down; careful not to stumble and drop the candle. I needed to sit down; my head had grown lighter and lighter, as though it was full of soft feathers. But I had to go on. I had to find my baby. I pushed open the door and as I walked into the room a darkness began to gather in front of my eyes. Queenie was there. She was running towards me and I was screaming. I couldn't stop. There were babies everywhere and I did not know which one was mine. Then the darkness closed in and Queenie's arms were around me.

45

Queenie

Queenie sat by Miss Swift's bed and held her hand. She didn't know what else to do. All night Miss Swift had been restless; slipping in and out of a fitful sleep. She was feverish and Mrs Waters had instructed Queenie to keep a close eye.

Queenie had expected the sisters to be displeased with her. She was afraid they would think she had acted out of turn by helping Miss Swift give birth. But Mrs Waters had seemed happy. She patted Queenie on the shoulder and said to Mrs Ellis quite proudly, 'She is learning well, our girl, is she not?'

Later on Mrs Waters had brought the baby downstairs and laid it on the sofa with all the others. She poured herself a glass of brandy and looked Queenie square in the eye.

'It is not so hard to help them get their babies out, is it? And the mother is fine. That is the most important thing with the ladies that come for their confinement. We need to send them home in good health.'

'Is Miss Swift to go home soon, then?' Queenie asked.

'I have sent word she has given birth and a carriage will be coming for her tomorrow evening. It is best she doesn't see the child again. I think the birth disturbed her more than is usual.'

Queenie remembered how Mam had been after the baby had died. Miss Swift had the same faraway look about her and she wouldn't stop crying.

'Your little one is fine,' Queenie kept telling her. 'She is doing grand and you'll be going home soon.'

'No!' sobbed Miss Swift. 'I cannot go. I cannot go without my child. Why did that woman take her from me? Please bring her back to me, Queenie. Please!'

Queenie felt helpless. She knew Mrs Waters would not allow it. 'I'm sorry,' she said quietly. 'But it is best you don't see her. It'll only make matters worse for you.'

'Then I will get her myself. She is mine! Nobody can take her from me!' Miss Swift struggled to get up. She sat on the edge of the bed and tried to stand.

'Please,' said Queenie. 'Stay in bed. You ain't well enough.' Queenie saw the splashes of high colour on Miss Swift's cheeks fade and her face turn a deathly pale. She looked like a wraith in a bloodied nightgown. Miss Swift stood for a moment, swaying on her feet. Then she went limp.

'Oh!' she gasped before collapsing back on the bed.

'I told you,' said Queenie. 'You ain't well.' She tucked Miss Swift back into bed and stroked the hair from off her forehead.

'My baby. My baby,' sobbed Miss Swift. 'Oh! What will happen to her?' Her eyes grew wide. 'All those other babies! Why are they all here? Have there been so many others like me?'

196

'Hush. Don't upset yourself,' said Queenie. 'They are all being looked after. And your little one will be looked after too.'

Queenie felt ashamed of herself. She wished she could bring Miss Swift's baby to her. It didn't seem right that Miss Swift wanted her child but was not allowed to have it. Her family had money. They would be able to feed another mouth. It was different for the other babies downstairs. They were either unloved and unwanted or *were* loved but their poor mams were destitute.

All day Queenie was up and down the stairs tending to Miss Swift and her other normal duties. She was fair worn out, but at least by late afternoon Miss Swift, apart from her distress, seemed much improved. She had taken some broth and the colour was back in her cheeks.

'The carriage will be here as soon as it is dark,' Mrs Waters said. 'So see that Miss Swift's bag is packed and she is dressed.'

Queenie took Miss Swift up a last bit of supper: a slice of ham pie and a baked rice pudding. She was out of bed and already dressed.

'Your carriage will be here shortly,' said Queenie. 'I'll help you pack up your things, shall I?' Miss Swift's face was like a cold stone carving. Queenie couldn't tell what she was thinking.

'Thank you, but I have already gathered together my belongings,' she said. Her hands were clasped tightly in her lap. 'And I have no need for any supper either.'

Queenie looked about the room. All of the few things Miss Swift had brought with her had indeed gone. Even,

Queenie noticed, the tiny chemises she herself had brought. Why was she taking them home? thought Queenie. It would do her no good being reminded of her baby like that. Then Queenie realised she was being unfair. Maybe they would be the only things she *would* have to remember her baby by.

'Just have a small bite of supper, won't you?' Queenie asked.' You'll be needing to keep your strength up.' Miss Swift didn't answer. She sat staring at the door and then a shudder ran through her body.

'Miss?' Queenie put her hand on Miss Swift's shoulder. 'What is it?' Miss Swift grasped Queenie's hand hard and pulled her down so they were face to face.

'You are my friend, are you not?' she asked.

'Course I am!' said Queenie. 'We're *good* friends, ain't we? You and me?'

'I hope so,' said Miss Swift. 'I hope with all my heart that it is true.'

'It's true,' said Queenie. 'Cross my heart it's the truth.'

'You need to help me, then,' said Miss Swift. 'I am taking my baby with me and you must help me to fetch her when the carriage comes.'

'What . . . what do you mean?' asked Queenie. 'What about your father?'

'I am taking her home with me,' repeated Miss Swift. 'She is the only thing worth having in my life. I will make Father see.' Her mouth grew tight with determination. 'I will make him understand.'

Queenie could see that Miss Swift would not be talked around. 'Right,' she said. 'I'll go and tell Mrs Waters, then. We'll get the baby wrapped up warm for you.' Queenie felt a slow fear creeping through her insides. She was afraid of what Mrs Waters would say and she was afraid of how things would be once Miss Swift had gone home. It was true, Miss Swift was her friend, the only one she'd ever had. She made Queenie feel like somebody and Queenie didn't want that feeling to end.

'No!' Miss Swift said, as Queenie went to leave the room. 'Wait! Do not speak to Mrs Waters. She will not allow it. I know she will not. We must surprise her with our intentions. You must bring my baby to me at the last minute.'

'But . . . but,' Queenie hesitated. 'I think it's best we let Mrs Waters know. I don't think she'll take on too kindly if we steal your baby from under her nose.'

'How can it be stealing?' asked Miss Swift. 'It is not her child to keep.'

'No,' said Queenie. 'But we'll still need her agreement. And . . . and there's something else.' She felt bad having to say what was on her mind. It seemed like nothing when she thought how Miss Swift must be feeling. But all the same, it needed saying. 'I'm sorry,' she said. 'I ain't going to be able to do what you're asking of me. Mrs Waters won't like me sneaking around behind her back one bit, and . . . and I need this job, and this is my home now.'

'I see,' said Miss Swift. 'So you will not help me, then?' She pulled her hand from Queenie's and lowered her head. 'I thought you were my friend.'

'I am!' protested Queenie. 'I am your friend.' Miss Swift could not know just how much she wanted to help.

'But you are still going to tell Mrs Waters of my intentions?' asked Miss Swift.

'No,' said Queenie. 'Not if you don't want me to. I won't. But I swear I'll help you as much as I can. I just ain't going to be able to fetch the baby as you asked.'

Miss Swift said nothing. She slumped back in her chair and crossed her arms over her empty belly. Queenie felt wretched. She knew she could do what Miss Swift asked. It would be as easy as pie. But she also knew she would be kicked out on to the streets for her trouble. She tried to think of another way to help. A way of getting Miss Swift in the carriage with the baby in her arms.

'Listen,' she said to Miss Swift. 'Listen to me. It'll be dark soon, and the carriage will be coming. Think hard. If we put our heads together I'm sure we can find a way!'

46

Ellen

I was sick with fear. I was weak and exhausted and still bleeding heavily. I fashioned a wrapping out of torn bed sheets. It felt thick and uncomfortable between my legs but I hoped at least it would keep the blood from flowing. My head felt loose and my whole body was trembling. All I wanted was my baby in my arms and to leave this place.

I was hiding in the bedroom along the landing from my own. I was standing with the door ajar listening for footsteps on the stairs. Queenie and I had decided what to do. It was the only thing we could think of in the short time we had. When the carriage arrived, Queenie was to take Mrs Ellis out into the backyard and distract her over some pretence. When Mrs Waters came to my room to fetch me, I was to run from this room, down the stairs and to the back kitchen to take my baby. Once she was in my arms there would be nothing anybody could do to take her from me.

I listened intently. All I could hear was the wind blowing down into the bedroom fireplace and my own heartbeat. I hoped I would be strong enough to hurry down the stairs as I would surely have to. The room behind me was in darkness. I had not dared to bring a candle with me for fear the light would be seen. Time seemed to have stood still and I was not sure how long I had been waiting, when I heard a distant knocking. There was a silent pause, then the muffled sound of voices. Had the carriage arrived at last? I took some deep breaths and readied myself. As I stared through the crack in the door on to the darkened landing, I saw candlelight flickering low down on the staircase walls and heard the soft tread of footsteps. She was coming! Mrs Waters was on her way to my bedroom. Her shadow appeared on the wall and grew larger and larger as she climbed to the top of the stairs. I shrank back into the room and held my breath as she walked past the door.

'Miss Swift?' I heard her say and the sound of one knock. Then I heard the click of a door handle and knew she had gone into my bedroom. Now I must move, I told myself. And quickly.

I stepped out onto the landing and walked swiftly to the stairs. A hot flush spread through my body and I felt my face grow damp with perspiration. Keep on! I told myself, and although my head felt odd – as though it was floating through the air on its own – I carried on down the stairs to the hallway and quickly made my way to the back kitchen. Mrs Waters was calling me.

'Miss Swift! Miss Swift? Where are you?'

Her voice grew louder and I knew she was heading back downstairs. My heart pounded with fright and the kitchen door in front of me swam before my eyes. But I was nearly there. My baby would be in my arms in a moment. I hoped Queenie had got Mrs Ellis out of the way. All I needed was a few seconds.

I opened the door and stumbled into the kitchen. Mrs Ellis was sitting in a chair by the fire. She looked up at me in surprise.

'Miss Swift! Your carriage is here. Mrs Waters is on her way to fetch you. Have you lost your way?'

Queenie was standing by the kitchen table folding linen. Her eyes were wide and she mouthed, *I'm sorry*, before bending her head back to her task. Panicked sobs began to rise in my throat. What had happened? Why had Queenie not done as she had said?

'Miss Swift?' Mrs Ellis said again. I looked wildly around the room. I could still grab my baby; Mrs Ellis would not be expecting it. I walked a few paces towards the sofa where the babies I had seen the night before lay quietly sleeping. Where was she? Where was my child? I stared at each bundle in turn. Which one was her? I could not make out her face among all the tiny features. The babies were too big or too small, and none had the tuft of black hair that I had caressed, only hours ago. Mrs Ellis was striding towards me.

'What are you doing, Miss Swift? Where is your bag? It is time for you to go now.'

'Where is my baby?' I screamed. 'Where is she?' Queenie ran and put her arms out to steady me.

'I'm sorry,' she whispered. 'There weren't nothing I could do.'

The kitchen door banged opened and I turned to see Mrs Waters enter the room.

'Ah . . .' she said. 'There you are. I have been looking all over for you. Now what's all this fuss about?'

I couldn't answer her; I could only stare in horror. I heard myself moan and the scene before me began to disappear in a grey haze. My last thought before all went black, was of my baby. My beautiful baby, who was cradled in the crook of Mrs Waters' arm.

It was cold. There was a chill creeping down the back of my neck. I felt movement. There were arms around me and I was being lifted. I opened my eyes and saw the night sky and blinking stars. There was a carriage in front of me, the doors open and my packed bag already inside.

'I knew you'd come round once the fresh air got to you. You just had a little swoon, is all.'

It was Mrs Ellis. She was to one side of me. My arm was flung over her shoulder and she was holding me around my waist. I turned my head and saw Queenie on my other side. She was holding on to me too.

'Queenie,' I managed to say. 'My baby . . . please . . .'

She shook her head slightly and looked straight ahead.

'Please!' I begged. 'Please!'

We were at the steps of the carriage and the driver came forward and held on to my arm. He was not one of Father's usual drivers. This one was unkempt, with long oiled hair that fell across his face. Mrs Ellis and Queenie moved away and the man gripped me hard around my middle. I still looked as though I was with child, my belly still tender and swollen, and I cried out in shock at the roughness of his handling. I thought for an instant to struggle free and run back to the house, but even as the thought flashed through my mind I knew it was useless to try. The driver grunted as he lifted me into the carriage with one movement. I landed awkwardly on the seat.

'Be careful!' I shouted. 'How dare you treat me like this. I will report you to my father!'

The man turned and sneered at me, showing a mouthful of blackened teeth. 'Little whore!' he hissed under his breath.

I felt as though he had slapped me in the face. Is that what I had become? An outcast? A nobody that could be insulted by the likes of this man? The thought did not shock me as much as it should have. I realised I had grown used to being a nobody. I was a nobody at home; I was undeserving of love and attention. Jacob had told me I was a nobody, and he had treated me as such.

'Goodbye, Miss Swift,' said Mrs Ellis as she moved forward to close the carriage door. 'I trust you will have a safe journey home.'

Queenie was standing behind her, looking downcast and nervous. Then a great thought struck me. I *was* no longer a nobody. I was *somebody* now.

I was a mother.

The thought filled me with pride and determination. Whatever happened tonight would not prevent me from being with my child. Nothing would stop me being a mother.

'Wait!' I said. 'Before I leave I would like to thank Queenie for attending to me so kindly during my stay.'

Queenie came to the door of the carriage. She looked up at me uncertainly. I reached out for her hand and quickly whispered, 'Listen . . . you must promise me that you will look after my daughter. Keep her safe. Come and let me know how she is. Come to the house on Bedford Square. The house with the horse-head door knocker. Ask for Mary. Please do this for me, Queenie. I will be back to get my baby. I promise you. As soon as I can.'

Queenie squeezed my hand in reply and I said in a louder voice, 'Thank you for all your kind attentions, Queenie. They have been much appreciated.'

Mrs Ellis came forward again. She nodded at me once and closed the carriage door. There was a jolt, I steadied myself on the seat, and the carriage was away.

I allowed myself to cry then. Great heaving sobs that tore at my insides. 'I will be back soon,' I sobbed into the darkness. 'I will be back for you soon. I promise.'

47

Queenie

'Well, she was an awkward one, all right,' said Mrs Ellis as the carriage pulled away. 'Glad to see the back of her.' She shivered. 'Come on. Let's get back inside. It's chilly out here.'

Queenie watched the carriage as it clattered to the end of the street, turned the corner and disappeared out of sight. She was filled with sadness as she stood there in the sudden empty silence. What had Ellen said? Bedford Square. The house with the horse-head door knocker. A long ago memory stirred inside her, but she could not quite grasp it.

Queenie followed Mrs Ellis back inside the house. 'Well, that's that,' Mrs Ellis was saying. 'A small nightcap now, I think. You can bring one up to me, Queenie. And a nice slice of fruitcake on the side.'

She went straight up to her room leaving Queenie to carry on down to the kitchen. That was it? thought Queenie. Another lady gone, another baby left here and all Mrs Ellis wanted was a slice of fruitcake. Did she not care? Did she and Mrs Waters not care at all? An image of the tin box under the bed flashed into her mind again and her skin began to prickle. She tried to push the picture away. There was an explanation for what she had seen. There had to be. A good reason that was not her business to know. She tried to think of other things: put the kettle on, pour a brandy, see where Mrs Waters had got to. They were good people, she kept telling herself. They were doing a good thing. Where would Miss Swift have gone if there weren't places like this to go to? Not even the workhouse would take in fallen women. And what of the poor babies? None of them stood a chance out there on the streets. Queenie knew what that felt like. No. The sisters did their best by everyone. Of course they did. And, Queenie decided, *she* was going to do her best for Miss Swift and her child.

The next morning began as always; Queenie rose early, got dressed and dragged her mattress back to the scullery. She stoked the fire, put the kettle on to boil and laid out two breakfast trays, one for Mrs Waters and one for Mrs Ellis. Then she checked on the babies. Miss Swift's little one was lying in a crate on her own. She was sound asleep; her lips pursed in a tiny pink kiss. Now and again they moved in a soft sucking motion. Queenie bent to kiss her head. 'Your mam'll be missing you something rotten,' she said. 'But not for long. She'll be back to get you soon, you lucky ducky.'

Queenie delivered breakfast to the two sisters, then came back to the kitchen to fix the babies' bottles. It was strange not having Miss Swift in the house. She missed her company and the thought of Miss Swift's empty bedroom filled her with a yearning for her friend. She hoped Miss Swift had made good with her father and would be back for her baby soon.

Queenie made up a jug of milk and lime and busied

herself sweeping while she waited for one of the sisters to come and add some drops of *the Quietness* to the mixture. A small wail broke through the sound of Queenie's sweeping. She crossed the room and saw that Miss Swift's baby was awake and wriggling. Her wails grew louder so Queenie quickly picked the baby up and rocked her gently to hush her. The sisters couldn't abide being disturbed by the noise of whinging babies. She must be hungry, Queenie thought. She hadn't yet had enough feeds for *the Quietness* to work. A small bottle won't harm. A quick one before the sisters came downstairs.

With the baby nestled in one arm, Queenie warmed some plain milk in a pan and carefully poured some in a bottle. Miss Swift's baby guzzled the milk down hungrily. Queenie held her close as she drank and listened out for the sound of footsteps. The baby's sucking grew less frantic and her eyelids began to droop back into sleep.

Queenie quickly tucked her back in the crate and willed her to stay quiet. As she ran her eyes over the other babies, she wondered which one would be next to go. How much longer before another disappeared in the night? She prayed Miss Swift would hurry and come back soon.

48

Ellen

When the carriage eventually stopped, it was Mary who opened the door to me. Her soft plain face, blotched by thread veins, and her kind grey eyes, were at that moment, the most beautiful of sights. We stared at each other, neither of us able to say a word. She held out her hand to me and I clung to her as she led me through the night-time drizzle into the house. Our silence continued as we walked into the hushed candlelit hallway and up the stairs to my bedroom. The house was warm and smelt sickly sweet; the over-powering scent of fresh flowers and furniture wax seemed almost to suffocate me.

I had forgotten how very quiet it was. We stayed silent until Mary had shut my bedroom door behind us. Even then we didn't speak. We held each other tight and sobbed as though our hearts would break. Mary kept pulling away to touch my hair, my cheeks and my arms; as though she did not know which part of me to try and mend first. Eventually she took a deep breath and wiped her eyes on the hem of her apron.

'Right then, miss!' she said, attempting to smile at me. 'Let's get you sorted out. Don't suppose you'd say no to a nice warm bath now, would you?'

I just nodded at her and kissed her cheek. I still could not bring myself to speak yet. There was too much to say and I was too exhausted to say it.

Mary had laid a bath sheet on the floor in front of the fire. My hip bath was placed upon it and I could see wisps of steam curling up from the surface of the water inside. A jug of cold water was next to the bath, a new cake of soap, a sponge and a pile of small linen towels.

Mary undressed me carefully. I saw her wince at the sight of my stomach. It was soft and spongy with long red lines etched deeply into the skin, as though I had been clawed by some wild beast. She removed the blood-stained cloths from around my lower parts as if it was a duty she performed for me every day.

I lowered myself into the bath water and felt the warmth seep into every part of me. It rolled slowly up my legs and wound itself gently around my stomach and breasts, soothing away the soreness and aches. Mary let me soak awhile before she lathered the sponge and began to wash me. I closed my eyes and let my body fall loose. I let her lift my arms to wash and I fell forward to let her soap my back. When I was clean all over, Mary helped me to climb out of the bath and she briskly wiped me dry. She had laid a nightgown out for me on the bed. It smelt so clean and felt fresh and crisp as it fell on my skin.

When I was tucked into bed, Mary came to sit beside me. She held my hand and she waited. Eventually I looked at her and said, 'I had a little girl, Mary. A beautiful little girl.'

She squeezed my hand as I told her all about my baby.

How she smelt like the sweetest of warm buns, the startling black of her hair and how wonderful those precious hours I had spent with her had been. Once I began to talk I could not stop. I told her about the dreary room I had spent the last few months of my confinement in. I told her of the sisters – Mrs Waters and Mrs Ellis – of how they repulsed me and made my skin crawl. And I told her all about my new-found friend, Queenie.

Mary kept quiet all through my outpourings. When I finished speaking, she looked at me solemnly and said, 'You have been through the greatest ordeal, miss. I can't imagine what it was like for you. But it is over now. You are safe and you are home. You must put it all behind you.'

'Put it behind me? Mary, I can never do that! I am a mother now. How can I ever forget my child?' As I said these words, I thought of my real mother, Dolly. How easy had it been for her to leave me? Had she felt like I did now?

'You must try to forget, miss. For your own sanity,' said Mary. 'Be happy your baby was born healthy and be glad that she'll be found a new home.'

'No Mary, no! You have not understood me!' My voice sounded shrill with indignation. 'I cannot return to life as it was before. I *had* no life before. I have found what has always been missing for me, Mary. I have found love. For my daughter. And I cannot let that go. Somehow I will have her with me. I swear to you, Mary, we will be together.'

Mary sighed, then smiled at me broadly. 'You don't know how much I was hoping you'd say that, miss!'

* * *

It was four days before Father called me to his study; a forlorn and grey morning. I had been keeping mostly to my bed, and apart from one time when I ventured to the library and suffered the sideway glances of the housemaids, I had seen no one but Mary. Now it was time to face Father.

Mary finished fastening my pink silk. My stomach had flattened a great deal and I could fit into my old gowns once again, but it brought me no pleasure.

'There,' said Mary, smoothing my skirts and standing back to admire her handiwork. 'You are ready, miss.'

I did not feel ready. My stomach had been churning all morning and I had not been able to take even a mouthful of breakfast. I kept remembering Father's face the night he sent me away. How he had looked at me with scorn and disappointment swimming in his eyes. He had made me feel like a piece of unwelcome dirt that had been brought into the house on the sole of his shoe.

A new feeling was growing inside me. It had started as a tiny hot seed planted deep in my heart. Now it was growing bigger all the time. I was filling with a rage that was rooted firmly in my heart. How dare Father treat me as he had! How dare he take me from my real mother and how dare he take my child away from me!

I strode to the door of his study at the appointed time of ten o'clock and knocked loudly three times.

'Come!' he said. At the sound of his voice I felt the anger inside me begin to shrivel and I concentrated hard on the memory of my daughter's face. I walked into the room and saw him sitting behind his desk, his face blurred behind a veil of cigar smoke.

'Ah! Good,' he said. 'We have been expecting you.'

We? I looked around and saw a figure standing in the gloom beside Father's unlit fireplace.

'Meet Edgar Rumble. A valued student of mine. He is proving himself most dextrous in the art of anatomical dissection.' Father gestured towards the figure, who stepped towards me with his hand held out. I could think only of the word *dissection* as I looked at the long thin fingers that were stretching towards me. I duly put my hand out and the stranger's hand felt like a cut of cold wet meat as it closed around mine.

'Most delighted to meet you, Miss Ellen.' His voice was soft. It slithered over me and my insides recoiled. I could not put an age to him, but already he wore the look of an old man, with thick moist lips and pale grey eyes that bulged from their sockets.

'Mr Rumble,' I said. I nodded my head in greeting and quickly took my hand away to wipe it secretly on my skirt.

'You are very fortunate,' said Father slowly. I looked at him. He had clasped his hands in front of his face and he was looking at me with an unblinking stare. 'Yes,' he said. 'Mr Rumble has agreed to take you off my hands. You are to be married next month.'

49

Queenie

It was Christmas Eve and Queenie had been to Wilkins Dairy to fetch a jug of fresh milk. She was in no hurry to get back to Wild Street now that Miss Swift had gone. She scraped her boots along the ground, not caring an inch that the shiny new leather got scuffed on the toes. There didn't seem to be much point to anything any more. Not without Miss Swift. She was missing her badly.

She was missing Mam, Da and the little ones too. She'd give anything to be going home to spend Christmas Day with them now. She still had the gifts she'd bought. She wouldn't care now what they thought of her turning up out of the blue after all this time. She wouldn't care if they'd missed her or not. She wouldn't be so proud now. Da would probably tease her about her posh togs anyway, 'Why, look at the little lady swanning in all la-di-da like,' she could hear him saying.

Chrismas Day would be nothing fancy, she knew. Perhaps a scrag-end of meat and some extra taters, but Da would make it seem like a meal fit for the Queen and would be smacking his lips and rubbing his belly. Queenie smiled to herself at the thought. Then something caught in her throat and she found herself rubbing away sudden hot tears.

She trudged along the last stretch of road leading back to Wild Street. Number 4 no longer looked so grand to her. The dirty grey walls frowned down on her and gave her the same sort of shivers that walking past Horsemonger Lane Gaol used to. Don't be daft, she told herself as she went inside. She listed inside her head all the chores she still had to do: rake the ashes, clean the grates, sweep the floors, bring in the coal and sort the laundry. That should take her mind off things for a time.

Mrs Ellis was in the kitchen and looked round sharply as Queenie came in the door. 'Ah, there you are,' she said loudly. 'We were wondering where you'd got to. Weren't we, Mrs Waters?' There was no sign of Mrs Waters in the kitchen. Queenie was beginning to wonder if Mrs Ellis had taken leave of her senses, when suddenly Mrs Waters appeared in the scullery doorway.

'Yes, Mrs Ellis. Indeed we were wondering. You were gone a long time, Queenie.'

Queenie was about to answer, when her attention was caught by the sight of a brown paper package tucked under Mrs Waters' arm. Her heart leapt and she couldn't help taking in a sharp breath as she stared. There was silence for a moment. Then Mrs Waters said, 'Whatever's the matter with you, girl? Have you never seen a parcel before? It's a Christmas gift for my niece. Now, what took you so long at the dairy?'

'Sorry, ma'am,' said Queenie, shifting her eyes away from the parcel. 'There was a big queue, ma'am. What with it being Christmas and all.'

'Humph,' said Mrs Waters. 'Well, now you're back, you'd better get moving. I want this place sparkling for tomorrow.'

'Yes, ma'am,' said Queenie, and she put the jug of milk she was still holding down on the kitchen table.

As soon as Mrs Waters had left the room, Queenie rushed over to the babies' sofa. She had got into the habit of counting them every day, and she knew straight away that one was missing. Her eyes flitted over each face and relief made her knees melt when she saw Miss Swift's baby still lying there with her eyes shut tight.

'Mrs Ellis?' she asked carefully. 'Has one of the babies gone to a new home?'

Mrs Ellis didn't look up as she mixed a bowl of stuffing for the Christmas bird. 'Yes, yes,' she answered absently. 'It was fetched while you were at the dairy.'

It was the answer Queenie had been expecting. It was what the sisters always said. Queenie wished with all her heart that it was true. She wished she could stop thinking such dreadful thoughts; of brown paper parcels and a tin box full of discarded baby clothes.

She looked at Mrs Ellis calmly mixing the stuffing. She didn't seem flustered at all. Maybe she *was* telling the truth. A baby fetched to a new home on Christmas Eve? What could be better? But a present for a niece? Queenie's thoughts whirled from one thing to another until she didn't know what to think. Just stop it, she told herself. Stop being daft. If she could have kicked herself hard, she would have done.

'Queenie?' Mrs Ellis called her over. 'How about, after you've finished cleaning, we mull some wine and bake a tray of mince pies for supper? It's Christmas, after all!'

She smiled at Queenie like an excited child, and Queenie

forced a smile back. 'That'd be grand, Mrs Ellis,' she said as she pulled out the broom to begin the sweeping.

Later that afternoon the kitchen was filled with the delicious smells of warm spices and baking pastry. Mrs Ellis was dipping her teacup in the pan of mulled wine and had become quite merry. She handed Queenie a cup.

'Go on, girl. Drink up now. And Merry Christmas to you!'

Queenie sipped at the warm liquid. It tasted as delicious as it smelt and as it slipped down into her belly, she felt her spirits rise. She and Mrs Ellis clinked their teacups together and Queenie took another gulp. It felt good. She was all warm and rosy. Things weren't so bad, were they? Here she was, having a fine old time on Christmas Eve. She had a job and coins in her pocket. She would take special care of Miss Swift's baby until she came back to fetch her. She would even go home soon, she decided. She would walk right in this time and never mind she'd been away for so long. If Da could get away with disappearing and be forgiven, surely she would be too?

She slid the tray of mince pies from the oven. The pastry had crisped just right around the edges and the mincemeat was bubbling gently. Her mouth watered, but she knew she'd have to be patient or she'd burn her tongue. She put the tray on the table to cool. Mrs Ellis was humming as she sat by the fire with another teacup of wine. Queenie fancied another drop herself, and with the mood Mrs Ellis was in, Queenie knew she wouldn't mind if she helped herself. She refilled her teacup, and as she carried it over to the table, the kitchen door opened and Mrs Waters stepped into the room.

'Sarah,' she said to Mrs Ellis. 'Can I have a word with you?'

'What? Now?' said Mrs Ellis. 'I've only just got comfy.'

'Yes, now,' said Mrs Waters over her shoulder as she left the room.

'Can't a soul have any peace?' grumbled Mrs Ellis as she pushed herself from her chair with an exaggerated groan. She swayed slightly as she stood and hiccoughed.

'Oops!' she giggled, putting her hand to her mouth. She winked at Queenie as she followed Mrs Waters out of the kitchen.

Queenie took a gulp of wine and again felt a delicious warmth spread through her body. She shivered with pleasure. Mrs Ellis had left her freshly filled teacup by the side of her chair. Queenie could see faint wisps of steam still rising from the warmed wine. Oh, but it'll get cold, she thought. Then it won't be half as nice. She picked up the teacup, thinking to take it to Mrs Ellis, and maybe Mrs Waters could fancy a cup too? She put Mrs Ellis's cup and another for Mrs Waters on a tray. No doubt they'd be in Mrs Waters' room, thought Queenie. She put a candle on the tray between the two cups and made her way up the stairs. She was feeling giddy from the mulled wine, and it wasn't until she was standing outside Mrs Waters' door, that she realised she should have brought a plate of mince pies too. She hesitated. Should she knock, or should she go back and fetch the pies first? Before she could decide, she saw that the door had been left ajar and she could hear every word the two sisters were saying.

'Stop whining, Sarah,' Queenie heard Mrs Waters say. 'I've told you. The fuss has died down. Have you seen any more about it in the paper?'

'Well, no. But I still think it's too soon. Can't we wait a while longer?'

'Listen, you silly cat, if we want to take more on, we need rid of some to make room. This lot are beginning to cost us; they've been here too long.'

'I know. But I'm so afraid we'll be caught out. What if they find the next one and trace it to us?'

'How can they? All babies look the same. Besides, I'll walk further this time and throw the parcel in the river. By the time anyone finds it, there'll be nothing to recognise anyway. And I'll do it tomorrow. There'll be nobody about on Christmas Day.'

Queenie's hands were shaking. The candle flame trembled wildly. She began to back away from the door as quickly as she dared. It was happening. The unthinkable truth that had been squirming away in the back of her mind had finally been spoken of. Queenie's head was reeling, her heart was pounding and her tongue had grown thick and dry with fear. The sweet smell of the mulled wine turned her stomach now. She swallowed hard and tried not to retch. She tiptoed back downstairs to the kitchen.

What was she to do? What in the Lord's name was she to do? She paced the kitchen, wringing her hands together. She couldn't bring herself to look at the babies. Poor mites. Being starved like that. And then . . . and then . . . She thought of the clothes in the tin box under the bed, stripped off poor, dead babies. She thought of the pink blanket she had pulled out – Little Rose's pink blanket – and the parcels Mrs Waters wrapped in the scullery. She shuddered. How many more had there been? She thought of all the babies that had come and gone. None of them taken away to new homes in the country. She thought of the strange hours Mrs Waters kept, of all the letters that went to and fro each week and of the ladies that came for their confinement and left their babies behind.

The truth had been under her nose the whole time. It horrified Queenie more than anything had ever done in her whole life. But what was worse, what was much worse was that Queenie realised she had known it all along. Deep down inside, she had known what was happening. She had known what the sisters were doing and she had chosen to ignore it.

50

Ellen

Married? Had Father just said *married*? The word sounded so ridiculous that I had to swallow a laugh that threatened to choke me. I glared at Mr Rumble, who was gaping like an ugly fish in the corner of the room.

'I am sorry, Father, but what did you just say?'

Father sighed impatiently. 'I said, Mr Rumble has kindly agreed to marry you. The ceremony is to take place next month. The twentieth of January, to be precise. Now, if you have any questions, please ask them quickly as Mr Rumble and I have important business to discuss.'

I swayed forward and gripped the edge of Father's desk. Thoughts and images were racing around my head. I saw a room full of babies and my own daughter's face squashed against Mrs Waters' bosom. I heard her cry for me and I felt the hollow space inside me where she had been. I saw Jacob's face, Mary's face, Queenie's face, and the wizened face of Eliza Swift, the woman I had always thought to be my mother. I saw all these faces swirling together in my head and the floor seemed to shift beneath my feet. I felt so feeble standing there in front of Father and it was hard to keep my anger from turning into fear.

'May I speak to you alone for a moment?' I asked in a low voice. I bit my lip to stop it from trembling.

Father raised his eyebrows at me. 'Whatever you have to say, you can say it in front of Mr Rumble. He is to be your husband, after all.'

Mr Rumble coughed. 'Yes, Ellen. Please speak what is on your mind.' He licked his lips. 'I hope we never have any secrets from each other.'

I gripped on to the edge of Father's desk even tighter. This could not be happening. Father was acting as though the last year had never happened. Was he honestly going to ignore the fact that I had just given birth to his first grandchild? Did he care how I was feeling? Did he care about what would happen to my daughter?

He was drumming his fingers on the desk. His eyes kept shifting to a pile of papers and I knew he had already grown tired of me. I was just a possession – a thing. A piece of business to be dealt with. All he wanted to do was to return to the papers in front of him and show Mr Rumble his latest sketch of a dissected lung or the four chambers of the heart. He did not care about his own daughter's heart. Anger and longing for my baby welled up inside me.

'Father,' I said, trying to keep my voice steady. I will not marry Mr Rumble. You cannot make me do this.'

Father stopped drumming his fingers. His neck flushed a deep red and the colour travelled quickly upwards, staining his jowls, cheeks and nose.

'You dare to question me?' he said. He laughed, but it was not a pleasant sound. 'And pray tell me. If you do not marry Mr Rumble, what do you plan to do with the rest of your life?'

'Well . . . well,' I stuttered. 'I would like to be reunited with my daughter.' I shot a glance at Mr Rumble. He did not seem the slightest bit disconcerted by my admission. He must already know. 'And . . . and, I should like to have some choice in the man that I marry.'

Father pushed himself up from his chair and leaned over his desk towards me. His whole face was now crimson and his jowls were trembling.

'ENOUGH!' he shouted. 'You have *no* choice in the matter. You have brought *disgrace* upon this family, and now you want to defy me when I have done everything in my power to hide your wickedness from the world?' He straightened up and took a deep breath. 'Mr Rumble has shown himself to be a highly honourable man in agreeing to take on a *fallen woman*. Did you think there would be men queuing up for you to choose from?'

Mr Rumble was looking at his feet. A strand of greasy hair had fallen from its place on his rather large head and I could see beads of sweat glistening on his forehead. I summoned up all my courage and looked straight into Father's eyes. 'But surely, Father, you disgraced this family first in the matter of my mother?'

Father clutched at his chest and droplets of spittle flew from his mouth as his lips formed words he did not seem able to speak. I had never seen Father lose control like this. I hoped I would not regret my words.

'You . . . you,' he spluttered.

Mr Rumble rushed to his side and proffered his hand-kerchief. 'Are you quite all right, sir?' he asked.

Father batted him away as though he were an annoying fly buzzing around his head.

'You,' he continued at me, his voice wavering with anger. 'You are clearly suffering from the very worst case of hysteria. You will speak no more of your lies and accusations.'

'Lies?' I protested. 'You know I am not lying.'

'BE QUIET!' bellowed Father. 'You leave me no choice. You will marry Mr Rumble and lead a good and quiet life and repent your sins, or I will have you committed to a *lunatic asylum*!'

I stumbled back as though I had been kicked by a horse. The only sound I could hear was Father's heavy breathing. 'But –' I began to say.

'BE QUIET!' he shouted again. Then in a more controlled voice he said, 'Do not forget, I am a highly respected doctor. Do you think anyone would question my diagnosis on the state of your mind?'

A shiver ran through me. He was right. I could think of no answer. All of the fight, anger and indignation drained out of me at that moment. I felt as weak and helpless as a newborn lamb.

'Go now,' said Father and he sat back in his chair and picked up a pile of papers.

I looked to Mr Rumble, but he was staring at the wall above the fireplace at something that was not there, his handkerchief still clutched in his hand.

'Out!' said Father.

I turned away from them both and as if in a trance, I opened the study door and walked out of the room.

51

Queenie

That Christmas Eve night was the longest of Queenie's life. Although she'd pulled her mattress out from the scullery and tried to get comfy, sleep just wouldn't come. She stared into the darkness for hours, her skin covered in goosebumps. She would have to fetch the coppers, she knew. It couldn't carry on. She couldn't stand by and watch more babies die. She couldn't see anything happen to Miss Swift's baby. It was murder, after all. *Murder.* The word filled her with dread. She could see it written inside her head in tall, black, heavy letters. In the small hours of the morning the heaviness of the word weighed her down, pinned her to the mattress and made her breathless.

As the light of dawn filtered in through the back window, she heard faint footsteps and the sound of the front door closing. She pictured Mrs Waters in her bonnet with the brown paper parcel hidden beneath her thick, black cloak. It was too late for that baby. She shuddered to think in which dark and lonely place the poor child would be laid to rest.

She should go now, she thought. Go and fetch a copper quick, before Mrs Waters got back and before Mrs Ellis rose from her bed. She lit a candle and pulled on her clothes. Her bones were aching with tiredness and her head was thudding. She checked on the babies first, praying none had passed on in the night. She put her fingers to each mouth and waited to feel the slightest touch of breath. All were well. Miss Swift's baby even stirred and let out a tiny whimper. 'I'm so sorry,' Queenie whispered to them all. 'I'm so sorry I didn't look out for you better.'

She hurried to fetch her shawl and as she wrapped it around her shoulders, a thought struck her. What would happen when the coppers came? What would happen to the babies? The workhouse, she realised with a shock. They'd be taken to the workhouse! When Miss Swift came back for her baby she'd be gone and there'd be no way of her knowing where to find her. Queenie didn't know what to do. She'd promised Miss Swift she'd mind the baby and once the coppers came there was no way of telling what might happen.

She had to let Miss Swift know. She had to go now and fetch her.

Before she had a chance to move, the kitchen door opened and Mrs Ellis walked in.

'You going somewhere?' she asked, looking at Queenie's shawl.

'No . . . no, ma'am,' stuttered Queenie. 'Was just feeling the chill, that's all.'

'Well, stoke the fire up then, girl!' She looked around the kitchen. 'You haven't even prepared the milk. It might be Christmas, but there's still work to be done!'

'Yes, ma'am,' said Queenie, and she busied herself making up a jug of watered-down milk and lime. Mrs Ellis added some drops of *the Quietness* to the jug.

'Have a quiet night, did you?' she asked Queenie.

'Yes, ma'am,' said Queenie. 'The babes were no bother at all.'

'Good, good,' said Mrs Ellis as she screwed the top back on to the sticky brown bottle of cordial. 'That's what we like to hear. Works wonders this stuff does.' She put the bottle back in her pocket. 'You can bring me my breakfast up when you've done with the babies.'

'Yes, ma'am,' said Queenie. 'And what about Mrs Waters? Will she need a tray taking up too?'

Mrs Ellis stopped before she got to the door, and without turning her head she said, 'No. Not yet I don't believe. She's just popped out to deliver some gifts. She'll be back soon, mind. You can take her tray up to her then.'

'Yes, ma'am,' said Queenie, seeing in her mind's eye a brown paper parcel left in the shadows under a railway bridge or sinking into the cold dark water of the Thames.

'Oh, and Queenie?'

'Yes, ma'am,' said Queenie, pressing her hands into tight fists.

'When you've done with the breakfast you can take the rest of the day off. It being Christmas and all!'

Mrs Ellis disappeared out of the door, crying, *Merry Christmas* in her wake. Queenie stood and watched the empty space where she'd been standing and slowly uncurled her fingers. She was a heartless creature all right, she thought. Trilling her *Merry Christmases* and all the while knowing what her sister was up to. Well, not for much longer. They would both get what was coming to them.

She looked back at the babies. Poor little creatures being

starved like that. There was no fat on any of their bones. Well, she would soon sort that out. She would feed them good and proper before she went to fetch Miss Swift.

She went to the pantry and fetched the freshest milk; the jug that was put aside for the sisters. Queenie smiled to see it had a layer of thick, yellow cream on top. She poured the lot in a pan with some crumbled loaf sugar and stirred it gently till it warmed through. She dipped her finger in and was glad to see how thickly it coated her skin. She sucked her finger clean. It tasted sweet and delicious and full of goodness. She would give some to each baby in turn and fill their bellies. There was plenty enough in the pan to go round. She worked quickly, and carefully poured the creamy milk into a bottle and pulled on a rubber teat.

She picked up the first baby and put the teat to its mouth. But it would not be roused. It lay floppy in her arms and no matter how she wriggled the teat it would not suckle. She lay it back down and tried again with the second baby. It was the same with that one. It was too weak and helpless to feed. She tipped a drop of milk onto her finger and rubbed it on the baby's lips. It still wouldn't wake up. Queenie shook it gently.

'Come on!' she said. 'Don't you know I'm trying to help you?' It was no good. Tears of frustration filled Queenie's eyes. She lay that baby back down too and turned to Miss Swift's baby. As she pressed the teat to her lips, the child stirred and her closed fists opened up like tiny flowers. Queenie squeezed a drop of milk onto the baby's tongue. She swallowed it and opened her mouth for more. After a few more drops, Miss Swift's baby took the teat in her mouth and began to gently suckle. Queenie sighed and closed her eyes. She held the baby close and thought of Mam and Da and the lost baby at home, and of all the other children that had passed through Wild Street. She had done nothing to help any of them. The huge feeling of shame that filled her insides brought tears to her eyes. She hastily wiped them away, not knowing if she was crying for herself or the babies.

She didn't hear the kitchen door open, so when Mrs Water bawled, 'What are you feeding that child?' Queenie jerked, and the bottle of milk fell from her hand.

52

Ellen

I sat in the library in a daze. Christmas Day and all hope had been snatched from me. I stared into the fire as though I might find some answers among the flaming coals. I was vaguely aware of a flurry of excitement in the house; like mice skittering beneath the floorboards. The servants were in a festive mood. No doubt Ninny had cooked up a goose or two with all the trimmings and was probably already celebrating with a glass of port. Downstairs there would be colour and laughter, chatter and life. Up here, it was just another cold winter's day.

Father's words turned over and over in my head. A lunatic asylum, or marriage to Mr Rumble? I could not imagine which horror would be the greater. The only asylum I had ever seen was Bethlem Hospital, or Bedlam as the servants referred to it. I had passed by its bleak grey walls and domed rooftop a few times when I was younger, on rare outings with one governess or another. I would be told to look away as our carriage drove past, but I would imagine I could hear the wails of the wretched inmates. One governess delighted in scaring the wits out of me and told me tales of poor unfortunates being chained by one leg or arm to a wall with only a blanket to hide their nakedness.

People would pay, in days gone by, she told me, to view these lost souls sitting in their own filth and to hear their haunting screams. Whatever went on inside that place, I knew I could not survive such a thing. And Mr Rumble? The very thought of him made my skin crawl. How could I be dutiful to a man who repulsed me so?

And what of my baby? There had been no chink in Father's armour. She did not exist for him. A sadness weighed upon me as heavy as the iron grey sky outside.

I stayed where I was, staring into the fire, wondering how my life had come to this. Even Mary did not seek me out. No doubt she was caught up in the preparations for Christmas dinner and in the task of dressing Mother for the feast. *Mother* . . . It was strange to think that I had ever believed I was part of that cold, brittle woman. She had made no attempt to visit me since my return or sent any word for me to attend her. If she knew I was aware of the truth, then she must be glad to call an end to all pretence. I did not miss her. I would be glad never to see her face again.

With every passing hour I sank deeper into despair. I could see no way out. If I left here to fetch my baby, where would I go and how would I live? I had no money of my own and no kindly relatives to call upon for help. Mary's sister came to mind. But I could not expect her to take in a stranger and her child with no means of paying my way. How could I ever earn a living? I had no idea what a woman could do out in the world. A servant or a governess, perhaps? But I knew without doubt that no one would employ me with a child in tow. I could go out and make my own way

233

in the world, but I would be unable to be with my child. The best I could do would be to pay another woman to bring her up and content myself with occasional visits. That I could not do. Realisation dawned on me slowly and painfully. With a heavy heart I made the most difficult decision of my life.

Hurried footsteps sounded up and down the hallway outside; servants carrying tureens and plates of steaming Christmas fare. The bell for dinner rang and I realised too late I had not prepared my dress or toilet. But what did it matter? My future was decided.

Mr Rumble was seated opposite me at the dinner table. He looked more repugnant in the light of a dozen candles than he had in Father's dimly lit study. Mother was sitting stiffly to my right. She was bedecked with jewels, feathers and fancy trimmings. She looked more dressed than a Christmas goose ready for the oven. Father was in his usual place at the head of the table. He carved the goose with precision and we watched as he delicately placed each sliver of fat-trimmed meat on a silver plate. I could not help but wonder if he applied such delicacy to the cadavers he carved up each day at the hospital.

Mr Rumble's gaze kept sliding towards me as his lips sucked on gravy and bone. He grunted as he swallowed each mouthful of food. Save for these sounds, there was silence as usual. I was barely aware of the food that passed my lips as I searched inside myself for the strength to carry out my decision.

With the forlorn affair finally over, we retired to the drawing

234

room. Mother and Father started a game of cribbage, and as I knew he would, Mr Rumble came to sit by me. His cheeks were aflame, reddened no doubt by the glasses of wine he had drunk at dinner. We sat in a heavy silence, watching Mother and Father, and I listened to the clock chime another hour. Mother soon tired of the game and insisted that Father escort her from the room. 'Excuse me, Mr Rumble,' said Father. 'I shall not be long.'

As the drawing room door closed, Mr Rumble dabbed at his forehead with his handkerchief. Now was my opportunity to say what I needed to say. I had to do it now before my resolve disappeared altogether. I turned to him and in a low voice I murmured, 'My apologies, Mr Rumble, for my earlier behaviour.'

Beside me, Mr Rumble jumped at the sound of my voice. 'Par . . . pardon?' he stuttered and took a gulp of his port.

'I said, I am sorry for my earlier behaviour. It was most rude of me, and of course I should be most honoured to accept your proposal.'

Mr Rumble coughed and a spray of ruby port landed on the front of his white shirt.

'Well, well . . .' he said, recovering himself. 'I knew you would come around to your father's way of thinking. It is better you marry me willingly, of course, but marry me you will. My career is on the ascent and I need a wife to take care of my domestic arrangements and provide me with a family.'

I twisted inside at these words and had to hold on to my seat to prevent myself from bolting from the room.

Mr Rumble straightened himself up and ran his fingers

235

through his hair. 'In return, your reputation can be salvaged,' he said. 'I will of course say nothing of your, shall we say, *shameful* past. If you do right by me, I am sure we shall be very happy.'

'But of course,' I said. 'I shall do my very best to be a good and dutiful wife to you.'

Mr Rumble grunted in reply.

My heart was pounding painfully. My future and that of my baby's rested on what I was about to say next. I took a deep breath and formed my face into what I hoped was a pleasing expression. 'And . . . and, I am sure in time I shall be able to grow very *fond* of you, as . . .' My voice shook. 'As I am sure you shall be able to grow fond of my child.'

Mr Rumble frowned. 'Your child?' he hissed. 'Have we not just agreed that no more is to be said of your shameful past?'

My mouth had grown dry and my words would not come easily. 'Of course we shall not *speak* of my past, as such, Mr Rumble. But you must see the advantages of a ready-made family which in time I am sure we can add to.'

Mr Rumble shook his head in confusion. 'Am I to understand that you expect me to take in your child as well as yourself?'

'Well, naturally. I cannot be separated from her, Mr Rumble.'

'Ha!' he spat. 'You think I would bring the shame of a *bastard* into my home?'

'But nobody need know,' I said, trying to keep my voice steady. 'In time we can let it be known that she is *your* child. There need not be any shame.'

'I think your thoughts must be addled somewhat, Miss Swift. Or else you have taken me for a fool.' He drained his glass of port and ran his tongue around his mouth.

It was all going hideously wrong. 'No . . . no indeed, I do not think you a fool,' I began.

He put his hand up to stop me from talking. 'Miss Swift,' he said patiently. 'It is all quite simple. I have made an agreement with your father to marry you. Your past behaviour and your child are to be entirely forgotten.'

I looked at his face and saw nothing but coldness and self-righteousness in the gleam of his bulging eyes. Was there any part of him I could appeal to?

'Mr Rumble . . . please,' I said and the tears rolled freely down my cheeks. 'Please . . . please, Mr Rumble. I will do anything you ask of me. Only please do not deny me my child. I beg you.' I reached out to grasp his hand, but he pulled away from me, a look of disgust upon his face.

'I have said all there is to say on the matter.' He stood up, taking his empty glass with him. 'And I assure you once we are married the subject will be closed forever.'

A fear so violent suddenly gripped my stomach. I ran from the room and got as far as the bottom of the stairs before I brought up my Christmas dinner all over the floor.

53

Queenie

'I said, what are you feeding that child?' repeated Mrs Waters as she stood in the kitchen doorway. She looked flustered and her orange hair was springing messily from out the sides of her bonnet.

Queenie bent down and scrabbled around to pick up the dropped bottle from the floor. Her face prickled with hot guilt. 'It's just milk, ma'am,' she said, sitting back up. Miss Swift's baby began to bleat. Queenie hesitated, not sure whether to put the teat back in her mouth or not. The cries grew louder and more insistent.

'Shut that brat up!' shouted Mrs Waters. 'Why is it crying, anyway? What is in that bottle?'

'I told you, ma'am. It's just milk.'

'I'm not stupid, girl. I can see it's milk. But it's not watered down, is it? Why aren't you using the proper mix?' She snatched the bottle from Queenie's hand and her eyes darted around the kitchen. Queenie saw them land on the big jug on the table that was full of the watered-down milk, lime and drops of *the Quietness*, and the smaller jug next to it full of creamy milk and sugar. Mrs Waters strode over to the table and looked inside both jugs. She dipped her finger into the smaller jug and licked off the drips. The

238

baby's cries changed to a constant wail. Mrs Waters turned to Queenie and looked at her hard.

'No wonder the child is mithering. What were you thinking of, girl? This stuff is far too rich, and how are we meant to keep them hushed without *the Quietness*?'

'I'm sorry, ma'am,' said Queenie.

'Sorry?' Mrs Waters banged her fists on the table. 'How dare you! How long have you been doing this behind our backs?' Mrs Waters was wild. Her eyes had narrowed to thin, black slits and her heavy bosom trembled with rage. Queenie hadn't expected this. It was all happening too quickly for her to think.

'I haven't, ma'am,' she stuttered. 'Honest. This is the first time I've done it.'

The baby was still wailing and Mrs Waters put her hands to her ears in frustration. 'Shut that child up!' She rushed towards Queenie and grabbed the baby from her arms. She flung the child over her shoulder and pulled the kitchen door open. 'Sarah!' she screeched. 'Sarah! Get down here!'

'What are you doing, ma'am?' Queenie was horrified. She stood up quickly. 'What are you going to do with the little 'un?'

Mrs Waters said nothing. She stood tapping her foot while the baby pressed its red screwed-up face into her shoulder and began to hiccough between sobs. Queenie heard the scurrying of footsteps and Mrs Ellis's shrill voice.

'What is it? Whatever is happening?'

Mrs Waters shoved the baby towards her. 'Just take it. Take the thing away from me. I can't abide its noise. If it doesn't stop soon, I shan't be able to account for my actions.'

Mrs Ellis did not question her sister. She looked at Queenie in puzzlement and then hurried away with Miss Swift's baby.

Queenie tried to stay calm, though her insides were turning over faster than a rolling barrel. Mrs Waters' heavy breathing filled the now quiet kitchen. The other babies were still sleeping. Not one had been disturbed by all the commotion.

Mrs Waters glared at Queenie. 'Don't you ever do that again. Do you hear me, girl? You disobey my orders again and you're OUT!'

Queenie looked at Mrs Waters. There was no hint of softness in her coarse face and no kindness in her angry eyes. Why would any mother hand their child over to a woman like her? thought Queenie. Those mothers had trusted this woman, had given her money to take care of their little 'uns. It weren't right, thought Queenie. It just weren't right.

She stood up tall and pushed her chin out. 'You can't talk to me like that no more,' she said. ''Cause I'm going anyway. Straight to the coppers.' It felt good to see the shock in Mrs Waters' eyes and to see her mouth go slack.

'What on earth do you mean, girl? You can't go to the police for a telling-off!'

Queenie snorted. 'I ain't going for that reason, am I?'

Mrs Waters shuffled her feet and crossed her arms over her bosom.

'Well . . . whatever do you want to be going to the police for, then?'

Queenie stared at her for a moment. There was no going back now. 'Where did you go this morning?' she asked carefully.

'Why . . . why . . .' Mrs Waters spluttered. 'That's none of your business, girl!'

'Well, I already know where you went,' Queenie spat the words out. 'You went to get rid of a poor, dead baby didn't you?' Queenie's voice cracked and she was dismayed to feel her eyes filling with tears.

Mrs Waters stayed quiet for a minute. Then she pulled her shoulders back and the hardness returned to her face. 'So what if I did?' she said.

Queenie was taken aback. The hairs on her arms began to prickle and stiffen. 'You . . . you murderer!' she whispered uncertainly. Then louder. 'I'll get the coppers on to you!' She started to move away, towards the back door.

Mrs Waters laughed: a soft, mocking sound. Queenie suddenly felt cold all over.

'And what would happen if you *did* bring the coppers here?' asked Mrs Waters with a half smile. 'What would you tell them? That some poor unfortunate babies died?'

'They didn't just die!' Queenie retorted. 'You starved 'em to death!'

'Listen,' said Mrs Waters, her face growing serious again. 'We just helped them along, all right? That is all. Sent them into the arms of Jesus. Do you not think they would have starved to death anyway, unwanted and out on the streets with mothers who can't provide for them? We just speed it along. Help those children find peace and help the poor mothers out in their time of need. You must see that can't be so very wrong?'

'But . . . but you get money for them! And you don't even give them a proper burial!' Queenie's mind was in a whirl. She thought back to the baby at home. It was true it had died of hunger; it had been so weak. But Mam and Da had loved it. And Da would have made sure it had a proper burial. She thought of him twisting his precious neckerchief round and round in his hands. 'You ain't sent any of 'em to new homes in the country have you? I'll tell the coppers that. I'll tell 'em you just dumped the poor little mites!'

Queenie was spitting mad now. But she was scared too. A wave of fear ran up and down her body. She wanted to get out quick, to run back home to Mam and Da and spill it all out. Maybe they would come to the coppers with her, and she would feel safe again?

Mrs Waters calmly untied her bonnet and put it on the kitchen table. She shook out her hair and began to untie her cloak. 'You run along to the police if you want,' she said, as she fiddled with the knot at her throat. 'But just you mind, girl. They find we've done anything wrong . . . then you're up to your neck in it too. You work for us don't forget. And no one will believe you didn't know what was going on. Shame for someone so young to have to face the hangman's noose.'

Queenie froze.

'On the other hand,' continued Mrs Waters, 'we could just carry on business as usual. You're a good little worker. You could join us and earn more money than you ever dreamt of.' She took off her cloak and put it over her arm. 'And don't forget,' she said, 'we are providing a good service. You think those mothers don't know what happens?'

Queenie couldn't answer. She was finding it hard to breathe, imagining a noose around her neck.

'I'll leave you to think it over, shall I?' said Mrs Waters. 'You'll see I'm right.' She picked up her bonnet from the kitchen table and, without waiting for Queenie's answer, she left the room.

Queenie sat down and put her head in her hands. Mrs Waters was right. She had known what was going on all along. She'd just closed her mind to it. Taken in by coins in her pocket and new boots and ribbons. She'd turned a blind eye. Even now, she was tempted by Mrs Water's offer of more money than she could dream of. It would all be so easy.

She groaned out loud again. Then she thought of Mam selling her body to feed their bellies. She thought of Tally, Kit and Albie and how just a crust of dry bread would make them smile. She thought of Da and her out on the streets selling apples. Everyone looking out for each other. She thought of Miss Swift begging her to take care of her baby. She thought of Miss Swift needing her baby, and her baby needing its mam.

Then Queenie was struck by a notion; a notion so plain and simple that it must have been there all along but she just hadn't noticed it. That was it, wasn't it? she thought. That was what it was all about. Being needed by someone was what made being alive worthwhile. Being needed by someone and looking out for them was more important than all the money in the world. Queenie stood up. She knew what to do now; she had a purpose and it felt real and proper and good. These babies all needed her, they all

243

deserved a chance. Miss Swift needed her too and, Queenie thought, whether they liked it or not, *she* needed Mam, Da and the little ones more than she'd ever needed them before.

Queenie walked fast. Every step that took her away from Wild Street made her feel lighter and safer. She prayed she hadn't left it too late for Miss Swift's baby. She headed straight for Waterloo Bridge and only stopped for breath when she was halfway over. She looked across the brown stretch of river at the hundreds of rooftops, smoking chimneys, church steeples and at the foggy outlines of fat grey buildings. Down in the river, despite it being Christmas Day, steamers and barges pushed through the water and Queenie heard the voices of the boatmen and the sounds of machinery. She looked along the bridge, back the way she had come, and she looked ahead of her towards home. Part of her wanted to stay where she was forever and not have to choose. But then she heard the sound of children's voices and she looked down to see a bargeman hoisting a small child onto his shoulders while another danced around his legs. She smiled to herself and set off walking again, knowing she had made the right choice.

Queenie stepped quietly through the doorway at home. They were all of them there, sitting around the fire with plates of steaming taters balanced on their knees. Mam saw her first. She dropped her plate on the floor and her hands flew to her mouth. Then Da turned to look and a huge smile spread across his face.

'My big gal!' he breathed. He was across the room in two strides and he lifted her from the ground and swung her around.

Then Mam was there covering her face with kisses and Kit and Albie were pulling at her skirts and singing, 'Queenie! Queenie! Queenie!'

Only Tally, all grown up and shy now, held back for a minute. But when Queenie held her hand out to him, he shuffled his feet, then grinned and rushed over to put his arms around her waist. Queenie was filled with peace. She knew she was home and she never wanted to leave again. Amid all the clamour, Queenie began to speak, and they gradually all quietened down and listened as she told her story.

54

Ellen

I could still taste the sour coating of vomit in my mouth as I lay on my bed feeling more wretched than I ever thought possible. Mary was hovering around me, unsure of what to say or do.

'I have to leave here,' I said weakly. 'I cannot stay and marry Mr Rumble.'

'But, maybe given time?' said Mary hopelessly. 'Maybe he will come round to the idea and accept the baby?'

I shook my head. 'No, Mary. Trust me. That will never happen. If I stay, I will never see my child again.'

'But miss,' Mary pleaded. 'Where will you go? How will you manage?'

I did not answer.

I will pack a bag tonight, I thought. And leave before the household rises in the morning. I knew there was a locked box in Father's study where he kept money to pay the staff wages. I would find a way to get into it. At least then, I could fetch my daughter and pay for a boarding house and food for a few days, until I could settle on what to do.

Mary looked distraught. 'Miss,' she said. 'You have no

idea what it is like out there in the world. I fear you will not survive. And I couldn't bear that.'

'I will not survive if I stay here, Mary. That is a certainty.' I needed her out of the way so I could begin to gather my belongings together and collect my thoughts. 'Mary, will you please leave me for a while?' I asked gently. 'I need to sleep a little.'

'Very well, miss,' she said, her eyes wide with worry. 'But promise me you will not do anything hasty.'

The lie slipped easily from my mouth. 'I promise,' I said. Poor Mary. I would miss her more than she would ever know.

She closed the door gently behind her. I rose from my bed. It was strange to think I would spend only one more night in it. I comforted myself with the thought that wherever I found to sleep after that, I would have my daughter with me. We would be together, and that was all I wanted in the world.

I lifted my gowns from the wardrobe. I would wear my oldest and dullest, I decided. I did not want to attract too much attention in the places I may be forced to go. My best dresses could be packed with my brooches and jewels. I hoped I could sell them and get a good price. My brushes, and my mirror too. I would no longer need them, but I would need every penny I could get. I rolled my gowns up tightly to make room for them in the carpet bag. I looked at my brooches. They meant nothing to me any more, and I began to wrap them in a petticoat. Suddenly Mary burst through the door. She looked a fright. Her face was drained of colour and her hand was shaking while it gripped the doorknob.

'Mary?' I rushed over to her. 'What is it? What has happened?'

'You'd better come quick, miss,' she said. 'There's someone here to see you.'

Someone to see me? Jacob's face flashed through my mind and my heart jumped into my throat. 'It is not . . . it is not Jacob, is it?' I asked.

'No, miss. No. It's the girl you told me about. It's Queenie, miss.' A strange expression crossed her face. 'And she's here with her mother.'

'Where are they?' I asked as I ran out of the door. 'She must have news of my daughter! Is everything well?'

'They are in the kitchen, miss. Ninny is giving them tea.'

I ran down the back stairs with Mary panting behind me. I prayed that we would not see Father, Mother or Mr Rumble. Mary caught up with me in the hallway. 'Something must be wrong,' I whispered to her fiercely. 'And why is her mother with her?'

Mary put her finger to her lips as we passed by the drawing room door. The strange expression passed over her face again and I knew there was something she was not telling me.

Queenie was sitting at the kitchen table with a pot of tea in front of her. She looked out of place and smiled at me nervously. Next to her was a dark-haired woman wearing the poorest of clothes. Beneath the grime on her face I could see she was fine featured with startling green eyes.

'Queenie!' I ran to her and she stood to greet me. I pressed her to me quickly. 'It is so good to see you,' I said. 'But what is wrong? Is everything all right with my daughter?'

'Miss.' Queenie greeted me. She seemed awkward and embarrassed and darted looks at Mary and at the woman who must be her mother.

'Queenie?' I was frightened now. What had she come to tell me? 'Please,' I pleaded. 'Is my daughter quite well?'

'She was well when I last saw her this morning, miss,' said Queenie hesitantly. She looked to Mary as if asking for help.

'Then if she is well, why are you here? What is the matter?'

'Miss,' said Mary, coming forward, 'I think it best you sit down a moment.'

I sighed in frustration and made a show of pulling a chair out and sitting in it heavily. 'Now. Will somebody please tell me?' Queenie's mother was staring at me as though I was an exotic exhibit. I wondered again why she was here. 'Well?' I looked at Mary in expectation.

Mary coughed. 'Miss,' she said. 'This is Queenie's mother.'

'Yes, I know that,' I said, nodding towards the woman.

'I didn't recognise her at first,' Mary continued. 'It has been a good few years since she worked here.'

I was confused. I looked at Queenie's mother, then back to Mary again. 'You are saying you used to work together? Well, I am sure that is a fine coincidence.'

'Miss . . .' Mary put her hands on my shoulders and looked me straight in the eyes. 'She was a maid in this house sixteen years ago. Her name is Dolly.'

My stomach flipped over. I thought I was going to vomit again. Dolly? The name was imprinted on my brain.

'She is your mother, miss,' said Mary gently. 'And none of us can quite take it in yet that she is here.'

There was a long silence. The words Mary had spoken would not stay still. They flew about the room and I could not grab hold of them.

Dolly Mother Dolly

Round and round the room they flew. I looked at Queenie. 'This is why you are here? You knew this all along?'

Queenie shook her head violently. 'No, miss. No! We came here for another reason, then Mam recognised the house and . . . and when Mary opened the back door . . .' Her words trailed off. Then her mother, who had not yet said a word, cleared her throat to speak.

'My Queenie here needed to see you about something dreadful and she asked me to come with her. I was fair shocked when she brought me here. Nobody ever knew about you, you see. Not my Queenie, not my husband, no one. Well, your Mary did, of course. It was her that was all for telling you just now. Said she would never forgive herself if she didn't let you know your own mam was sitting downstairs in the kitchen. It's a shocker, I know. I reckon my Queenie's as floored as you. Finding out she has a sister and all.'

She paused for breath. I stared at her dark hair that was the same shade as my own and Queenie's, and at her nose that was as straight as mine.

'I never forgot you,' she said. 'I always wondered how

you were doing. I would walk here sometimes, you know, and stand in front of the house and watch. Sometimes, if I waited long enough, you'd be brought outside for a walk. I could see how big you'd grown and how pretty you were. And such a lady! I talked to you once when you were a little 'un. Do you remember?'

I shook my head. All those years she had been there; close by, watching me, and I had never known.

'I remember,' said Queenie suddenly. 'I remember the horse-head knocker on your front door! And I remember you! You were wearing a white dress with yellow flowers on it. You had a long yellow ribbon in your hair. I thought you were the loveliest thing I'd ever seen.'

Dolly raised her eyebrows at Queenie in surprise.

'You took me with you once didn't you, Mam?' said Queenie. 'I never forgot it. It was a hot day. You bought me an orange to suck on.'

'Well I never!' said Dolly. 'Fancy you remembering that!'

It was so peculiar to hear myself being spoken of like this. The woman was my mother! She was Dolly. Although I had wished so hard to meet her, now she was sitting in front of me, I did not know how to feel. And Queenie. My sister. I kept looking from one to the other. My mother, my sister. I began to tremble, from shock or fear or happiness, I did not know.

Then everyone fell silent. There were too many questions and too many answers to be spoken. Queenie was shifting nervously in her chair. Suddenly, she pushed her teacup to one side, and stood up.

'Ellen,' she said. 'You have to come with me back to

251

Wild Street now. You have to get your baby out of there. That's what we came to tell you. We have to hurry. And me Mam is going to fetch the coppers.'

She turned to her mother, *our* mother, I realised with a jolt, and I saw the look of a fearful child pass across her face as she said, 'You'll tell them how it really was, won't you, Mam?'

55

Queenie

Evening had fallen cold and frosty by the time Mam set out to fetch the coppers and Queenie hailed a cab to take her and Ellen back to Wild Street. Ellen had fallen into a strange and silent state since Queenie told her of Mrs Waters, Mrs Ellis and the brown paper parcels. The maid Mary wept hysterically and then wrapped Ellen in a warm cloak and pressed another one upon Queenie. Queenie had never worn anything so warm before. It was like being covered in a dozen soft blankets. She imagined, with a flicker of pride, that any stranger seeing her and Ellen together in their cloaks would straight away know they were sisters. She wanted to talk to Ellen about it. She wanted to hold her hand and feel close and know that everything was all right. But that would have to wait.

Queenie asked the cab driver to let them off around the corner from Wild Street, and now she felt the horses begin to slow.

Queenie stepped out of the cab into the quiet of the street and waited for Ellen to follow. She handed the driver some coins and asked him to wait.

'We won't be long,' she told him. Queenie pulled her cloak around herself and motioned to Ellen. 'We'll go round the back,' she whispered. 'Through the back door into the kitchen. We'll be in and out before anyone notices.'

Ellen nodded. Her eyes were wide and staring and her face looked white as milk. They walked silently round the corner, into Wild Street and past the front railings of number 4. They turned down the passageway that led to the back of the house. The winter moon was so pale that its light didn't reach into the shadows and Queenie trod slowly, taking care not to stumble. The narrow passage was piled high with dried, cracking leaves and broken twigs, blown in and forgotten since autumn. As Queenie crept forward she stepped on a twig. Her heart flew into her throat and she froze as the air filled with a noise that seemed as loud as a whip crack. Ellen grabbed on to the back of Queenie's cloak and they both stood rigid, not daring to breathe. There was no sound and no movement from inside the house. Queenie's heart slowed to normal. Mrs Waters and Mrs Ellis would probably be half drunk on Christmas brandy by now and would most likely be snoring in their chairs.

She stepped forward again, scrunching the leaves beneath her boots. Queenie felt the tremble of Ellen's hand as she kept a tight grip on the back of her cloak. They reached the back door and Queenie turned the handle slowly, praying it wouldn't be locked. There was a sharp click and Queenie let out a small sigh of relief as the door opened inwards.

The kitchen was in darkness. Queenie couldn't see a thing. Not even the faint glow of a dying fire.

'Wait here,' she whispered to Ellen. 'I'll find a candle and some matches.' She put out her hands and touched the cold walls. Slowly and carefully she felt her way into the kitchen and along to the shelf by the scullery door where spare candles and a box of matches were kept. She rolled two candles into her hand and with shaking fingers she lit both with one match. She carried them back to where Ellen stood waiting just outside the door and put one in her hand. Ellen's face was still drained of colour, and she still hadn't spoken a word.

'Come on,' said Queenie. 'It'll be all right. Let's be quick now. Let's get the baby and be out of here.' She held out her hand to Ellen and pulled her gently into the house.

The candle flame threw a soft glow of light into the kitchen. Queenie could see the sofa across the other side of the room and the lumps and humps of the wrapped-up babies. She couldn't believe it was gong to be so easy. She crept nearer and reached out to the first bundle. Her hand flattened the pile of rags into nothing and her guts jumped into her mouth. The bundle was empty. There was no baby. She quickly felt along the rest of the sofa. It was all just rags and cloths and old blankets. Behind her, Ellen whimpered. Oh Lord, thought Queenie. Not all of 'em. Please to God, not all of 'em.

'Where is she?' whispered Ellen. 'Where is my child?'

'I don't bleedin' know,' said Queenie fiercely as she heard Ellen's whimpers turn to frightened sobs. She pressed her own lips tight together to stop a scream of frustration from escaping into the shadows of the kitchen.

Queenie held her candle at arm's length and swept it around the room. She shone the light on the door to the cellar, the table, chairs and empty crates. She turned on her heels towards the fireplace and there was the back window and the scullery door and . . . suddenly she screamed and dropped the candle on the floor.

'Sneak into my house, would you?' said a voice.

Queenie couldn't move. How could they have missed her? She heard short rasping breaths and a thick cough. She picked up her candle, which was spluttering but still alight, and held it out towards Mrs Waters, who was sitting in a chair pushed close to the cold fire.

'And who is this with you?' Mrs Waters voice was slurred, like Da's used to be after a night on the beer.

'You know who she is,' said Queenie. 'It's Miss Swift. She's come to get her baby.'

'Miss Swift, you say?' Mrs Waters laughed nastily. 'Never seen her before in my life.' She took a long swig from the bottle in her hand. 'And what baby? There's no babies around here.'

Mrs Waters was in a right old state. Queenie could see that. Her face was mottled with red and purple patches and spit dribbled from the edges of her lips. Queenie looked at her as though for the first time, and knew for certain she was standing in front of a monster. If Da was here he would've knocked her right off that chair.

'What have you done with 'em?' she asked. 'What have you done with the babies? I've fetched the coppers, you know. They'll be here soon.'

'I wondered if you really would. You nasty cat.' Mrs Waters belched loudly. 'Well, there aren't any babies. They're gone.' She closed her eyes. 'Gone, gone, gone,' she sang to herself. 'Into the arms of Jesus.' She chuckled and lifted the bottle to her mouth again.

Suddenly, Ellen pushed Queenie to one side and stepped forward. 'Where is my baby?' she screamed at Mrs Waters. 'What have you done with her, you evil old woman?'

Mrs Waters smashed the bottle on the floor. She picked up the jagged remains and tried to push herself up from the chair. She was a hefty size and she swayed from side to side as she stared at Queenie and Ellen with eyes that were like pieces of hard, black coal. Queenie looked about frantically for something . . . anything to grab in case Mrs Waters went for them. There was only the poker by the fire and Mrs Waters was standing right next to it. The whole of Ellen's body seemed to be trembling. But she stayed where she was and stared hard at Mrs Waters. Hot candle wax dripped onto Queenie's hand, but she didn't flinch.

'You get out of my house,' hissed Mrs Waters. 'There's nothing for you here. No babies. No nothing.' She flung her arm out, still holding on to the broken bottle, and pointed towards the back door. 'Get out!' she slurred. 'Let the coppers come if they want. They won't find anything here.'

'We're not going anywhere,' said Queenie. Her voice was loud and strong. She felt hard as a poker herself, and red hot with anger. She wasn't going to be scared off that easy. The coppers would be here soon, she was sure of it. Mam had gone straight to fetch them. Then Mrs Waters would get what was coming to her. Babies or no babies. Queenie would tell the coppers everything.

Just then, Queenie heard a small noise. It was far away

257

and muffled, but the tiny sound made her prickle all over. She turned to Ellen and could see by the wideness of her eyes that she'd heard the noise too. The tiny sound grew louder. Queenie saw Mrs Waters cock her head and glance towards the cellar door. She had heard it now too.

'Get out!' Mrs Waters suddenly screamed again. She threw the broken bottle and a shard of glass sliced across Queenie's cheek. Queenie cried out in shock. A warm wetness began to drip onto her shoulder.

'It's a baby!' whispered Ellen, still listening closely. She grabbed Queenie's arm and squeezed it tight. Queenie's cheek was stinging like mad now.

'You've hidden 'em in the cellar!' she said to Mrs Waters. 'Couldn't risk dumping 'em all at once, could you?' Queenie stepped towards Mrs Waters, so close she could smell the brandy on her breath. 'Bet you dosed 'em up good and proper too,' she said. 'Didn't expect any of 'em to make a noise, did you?'

Mrs Waters took a faltering step backwards. Her face turned the colour of uncooked pastry and she was breathing heavily. 'Should never have taken you in,' she panted. 'Knew you'd be trouble.' She sat heavily in her chair, muttering nonsense to herself, her head falling forwards onto her bosom.

Queenie ran to the cellar. She tugged at the door and twisted the handle from side to side. It was locked tight. She couldn't hear the crying any more. It had stopped. The poor babies. Lying down there in the cold, damp darkness with not even a blanket to keep 'em warm. Ellen ran up beside her and began to twist at the handle too.

'Where is the key, Queenie? We have got to open this door!'

Queenie's mind was whirling. Where did Mrs Waters keep the keys? She couldn't think.

The kitchen door suddenly creaked open and the tremulous voice of Mrs Ellis whispered loudly, 'Margaret! Are you there? I heard noises. Is everything all right?

Queenie went rigid. She looked at Ellen and put her fingers to her lips. Mrs Ellis moved further into the kitchen. Queenie pressed herself into the shadows by the cellar door; Ellen close beside her.

'Margaret!' Mrs Ellis was shaking her sister. 'What was all that noise I heard?'

Mrs Waters opened her eyes slowly and looked blearily at Mrs Ellis. Then suddenly her eyes widened, she sat upright and pointed a finger towards the cellar door. 'They're in here, Sarah. Look! They're in here and causing trouble!'

Mrs Ellis turned round quickly, her hand clutching at her throat. She stared at Queenie. 'Has she called the police?' she hissed over her shoulder to Mrs Waters.

'Says she has,' Mrs Waters slurred. 'They know where the babies are too. One of them squealed. You didn't give them enough of a dose, did you? You stupid mare!'

Mrs Ellis turned white. She began to whimper, 'We're done for! Oh God, we're done for!'

'Shut up your whining!' shouted Mrs Waters. She pushed herself up from her chair and grabbed the poker. Something clanked as she began to stumble towards Queenie and Ellen. 'The keys!' said Queenie, suddenly remembering. 'They're in her skirts!' Before she had time to think any more, Mrs Ellis rushed towards her and grabbed her arms.

'What have you done? What have you done?' she screamed at Queenie. 'We trusted you!' She let go of one of Queenie's arms and reached out to scratch her face. Tears of pain sprang to Queenie's eyes as Mrs Ellis's nails dug into her already cut cheek. She twisted her arm out of Mrs Ellis's grip, and with a huge yell she shoved Mrs Ellis hard in the belly with both hands. Mrs Ellis stumbled backwards and fell against the kitchen door. Queenie readied herself to punch again. As Mrs Ellis pulled herself up, Queenie tightened her fists. Mrs Ellis looked shaken and terrified. Instead of coming at Queenie, she opened the kitchen door and fled up the stairs.

There was a thump and a cry from behind. Queenie whirled round. Ellen's candle was lying on the floor and Queenie could see the dark shapes of flailing arms and legs on the floor by the fireplace. Mrs Waters was grunting and squealing like an excited pig and Queenie saw the orange of her hair spread across the hearth. Had she got hold of Ellen? Was she trying to throttle her? Before she had the chance to get back across the kitchen, there was the rattle of metal and Ellen shouted, 'I've got them, Queenie! I've got the keys!'

Queenie could hardly believe her eyes. Mrs Waters was sprawled on the floor and Ellen was leaning over her dangling a huge bunch of keys from her hand.

Queenie snorted in disbelief. 'You're a dark horse, Ellen Swift,' she said. 'But I ain't half glad you're my sister.' She helped Ellen up and they both looked down at Mrs Waters.

She had gone limp and seemed to have fallen into a drunken stupor. Queenie laughed and Ellen smiled weakly, then they hugged each other tight.

'Quick now,' said Queenie. 'Let's fetch your baby.'

Queenie tried each key in turn, guiding them into the rusty lock: silver keys, brass keys and long iron ones. Her hands were shaking as she fumbled about. Ellen kept whispering, 'Hurry, hurry,' and Queenie was about to throw the keys at her in frustration when there was a loud clunk and the cellar door swung open. Cold, stale air hit Queenie in the face, but there was not a sound to be heard from the black hole. Ellen plunged her candle into the darkness and began to make her way down the stone steps. Queenie lifted her skirts to follow behind.

Suddenly there was a bang and the kitchen was flooded with light. Queenie turned to see Mam and a couple of stern-faced coppers wrapped in capes, shining their Bull's Eye lanterns into the room and onto the body of Mrs Waters splayed out in front of the fireplace.

56

Ellen

The stone steps that led down to the cellar were slimy and wet and seemed to go on forever. The air grew colder and I shivered violently when I thought of the children down there. How long had they been hidden away? I prayed the rats had not found any of them yet. I prayed the cellar had not become the most terrible of coffins. I did not stop to look around when I heard noises in the kitchen above. I needed to get my daughter out of this dark place as soon as I could.

Sticky cobwebs drifted across my face, and I saw the walls either side of me were black with mould. The further I descended the more foul the air became. Soon I could taste it, thick and sour, on the back of my tongue.

At last I reached the bottom step. My candle lit up a small circle of glistening soil. I lifted the candle and the circle grew bigger, lighting up a mound of rubbish piled up against the back wall. There were broken pans, garden tools, an iron bedstead and a row of splintered, wooden fruit boxes.

I heard more thuds and shouts from above. Then a male voice echoed into the cellar.

'Miss? We'll have you up here now, if you please.'

The words passed over me, like a far-off voice in a dream.

I was staring down into the fruit boxes, and what I saw made my heart shrivel into itself. Little bodies, like scraps of humanity, lay two and three in each box. I could not breathe. I could not blink. I could not move. They were all skin and bone with barely a stitch on any of them, and they were lying as still as porcelain dolls. I picked one up and held it in the crook of my arm. It was as light as a feather and I could not tell if it was still alive. I needed to get it out of here. I needed to get them all out.

Then I saw her at the end. In the last box. It was her hair I recognised. The soft black tufts. I heard a moan. Was it my own? Then I heard a voice again in the distance.

'If you don't come up now, we shall be forced to come and get you.'

With my free arm I scooped my daughter up gently. She felt so cold and so delicate, I thought she might break. I held her close, rocking her gently. I put my cheek to her mouth. I felt nothing.

'Please,' I begged her. 'Please don't leave me. I am here now. I have come to get you like I promised.'

Then a miracle happened. As a heavy hand clasped my shoulder, I felt her breath as soft as a whisper on my cheek.

Then the voice came again; loud and by my side.

'Oh Lord! Oh Lord!' it said. 'Sir! You'd best send for help. They're all down here and I don't know if any of them's alive.'

I could not let go of either baby. The man tried to take them from my arms before he led me back up the stairs. But I would not let go. He held on to my elbow and we walked up to the kitchen. I heard Mrs Waters screaming.

'Get your hands off me! I've done nothing wrong. No! Leave me be!'

The kitchen was full of policemen with worried faces. Two of them were dragging Mrs Waters out of the door. Dolly was there too, with her arm around Queenie's shoulder.

'Please, sir!' Dolly was pleading. 'The girls have done nothing wrong! You can't take them away!'

'Out of the way, ma'am. Or I'll have to take you to the station too.'

'But sir! We only came to rescue my own granddaughter. Look! Here she is now!' Dolly came running over and put her hands to her mouth when she saw the babies in my arms. 'Oh! The poor little mites,' she exclaimed.

There was confusion and crying. The other babies were brought up, one by one, from the cellar. 'This one's gone,' someone said. I saw Mrs Ellis, standing by silently. She looked like a bewildered, lost child. I heard words flying around the room and disappearing out of the door. *Workhouse . . . doctor . . . wet nurse . . . murder . . .*

A man smelling of leather and authority came and prised the babies from my arms. 'This one's gone too,' I heard someone say.

Then I was taken outside. The cold air slapped me in the face and crept under my cloak as I was pushed up the steps of a cab with blackened windows and bars at the door. Mrs Waters was inside already, lolling back on the wooden seat. Queenie was there too. She reached out for me and we held on to each other and watched as Mrs Ellis was bundled in after us and the door was closed and locked.

'Where are they taking us?' I whispered to Queenie. My teeth were chattering; my whole body trembling with dread.

'To the cop house,' said Queenie. 'But don't fret. Me mam will look after your baby and we'll be out of there as quick as a wink as soon as we've explained ourselves.' She squeezed my hand.

Then Mrs Waters laughed loudly, as though she had heard the funniest thing. 'You stupid girls.' She snorted through her nose and laughed again. 'We're all going to swing for it. Don't you realise? We're all going to swing for it.' And she began to cackle like a mad woman.

I have been a week in this cell now. I have grown used to the bare whitewashed walls and the narrow slit of light from the window above my head that is my only glimpse of the outside world. It is not so bad.

Mary has visited me often and brought me clean clothes, plenty of books and newspapers to read and baskets from Ninny full of her bread, pies and off-cuts of meat. The newspapers are full of the whole business. It is shocking to see my name associated with such horror.

THE MORNING ADVERTISER

South Westminster District Bench – Saturday
Before Mr. F.B. Parfitt (in the chair), and Mr. H.M. Wallis

CHILD MURDERERS ARRESTED

Margaret Waters, 45, Sarah Ellis, 43 and Queenie O'Connor, 15, of No. 4, Wild Street, St. Giles-in-the-Fields were charged with having between March and December 1870, feloniously killed and murdered certain children unknown. Ellen Eliza Swift, 16, of No. 22, Bedford Square, Bloomsbury was charged with being an accessory after the fact. It will be remembered that after the prisoners had been taken into custody, a number of pawnbroker's duplicates were found in the possession of Waters and her fellow prisoners. A pawnbroker's shop in Southampton Street Road, not far from the 'baby farm' in Wild Street, was visited, and in the months between March and December there was discovered to have been pledged a number of articles of children's clothing, including thirteen shirts, four long white petticoats, five chemises, twelve infant nightgowns, eight infant napkins, a child's black velveteen jacket and a number of frocks and blankets. There are other articles yet in pledge to be examined, but it is anticipated that further light will be thrown upon the shocking transactions of the prisoners. Yesterday likewise was discovered the body of another infant near St. Giles' Cemetery.

THE MORNING ADVERTISER

INQUEST HELD

Last evening Mr. Carter held an inquest at the St. Martin's workhouse touching the death of a male infant brought from No. 4, Wild Street, St. Giles-in-the-Fields, to the workhouse. The Coroner said that he need not remind the jury that a short time previous to the death of that child, a number of children had been found by the police in the house situated at No. 4, Wild Street. Dr. Bullen, workhouse surgeon, deposed that the deceased died from congestion of the brain, with effusion into the ventricles, connected with intermittent diarrhoea. The congestion of the brain had been brought about by want of sufficient food.

Verdict – 'Death from starvation'

I could only bear to read two articles. I have asked Mary to stop bringing the newspapers now.

Mary tells me that Little Queenie (for that is the name I decided to give my child) is thriving. My mother Dolly has been taking great care of her. She will bring her here to visit me soon, if I am not released beforehand. Some of the other babies did not fare so well. Those that survived have been taken to the workhouse. Mary is hopeful that good homes will be found for them.

I hear that Father has spoken out for me and has given evidence on my behalf. My only involvement in the dreadful business was that I gave birth in that house of horrors. Mary tells me that when the court meets next, my case is sure to be dismissed and I will be free to go. Father has been brought low by the scandal. A number of journalists have written scathing articles about him in the press. He sent his solicitor to see me; a thin, nervous man called Mr Danby. He would not look at me as he informed me that Father was willing to pay me a one-off sum of two hundred pounds if I cut all contact and agreed never to speak of the whole matter again. It is the final insult, the final proof that he never loved me. I am glad Father has suffered; I hope he suffers more. I will take the money he has offered me, if only for Little Queenie's sake, and hope never to see him again.

It is hard to sleep in this place at night. Even though Mary sent me a thin mattress, the wooden bench I lie on still leaves me bruised and sore. There are dreadful noises at night too: rattling, banging, wailing and shrieking.

I have found a way to some peace, though. I imagine the small house I will buy with Father's money. Maybe a cottage out in the countryside somewhere, where Little Queenie can run about in the fresh air. Mary will come and live with me, and Dolly, her husband and the boys will visit often. I plan on buying a market stall for them.

I think of my sister Queenie all the time. Mary says the whole of London is talking about the murders. The police are still finding bodies. Some parcels have been dragged from out of the Thames. Mary says the courts are taking a dim view of Queenie. They do not believe she knew nothing of the business that was going on under her nose.

I pray for her every night.

57

Queenie

Queenie sat hunched in the corner of her cell with her knees drawn up to her chin. The cold of the stone floor seeped into her bones. She hardly noticed the pain. She couldn't feel much of anything any more. The day passed slowly. Like every other day during the past few weeks. Each hour plodded along endlessly, like a worn-out carthorse on a treadmill. Queenie prayed for darkness to fall so she could escape into sleep. But she knew when night did eventually come, she would wish it never had. She knew that each finished day brought her closer to the end.

Her solicitor, Mr Wood, had told her over and over that he would do his very best by her. She was an innocent in all of this, he would tell the court. She worked only as a maid. How could she have possibly known the extent of the dreadful trade in babies that was being plied by her employers? He would do his best, he kept saying, but it would be a hard case to fight. She should prepare herself for the worst. The newspapers were full of it. The public were outraged and witnesses had come forward. Mr Epps the chemist and another chemist on Duke Street were both to swear on oath that she had purchased Godfrey's Cordial from them on a number of occasions. A clerk from the post office on Drury Lane was also to swear she had bought brown paper and string.

Queenie didn't want to hear these things. But she knew Mr Woods was only being honest with her. Mr Woods used big words and Queenie didn't understand what he meant by things at times. But he was a kindly man. She liked his clever voice and the way he tugged at the corner of his yellow moustache when he was trying to explain something to her. She liked his checked wool suits which smelt of tobacco and dust. He once showed her a photograph of his pretty young wife and baby daughter. Queenie thought that was a very brave thing for him to do. It was after that she decided she would trust him to look out for her.

Queenie had never thought much about God before, but now she was made to think about him every day. The prison chaplain wouldn't leave her alone.

'Search your heart for the truth,' he told her. 'God will forgive you your sins if you only confess.'

But what should she confess? She knew what she had done and she knew what she hadn't done. And she hadn't killed any babies. God would know that because it was the truth. God could see everything, the chaplain told her. Even what was in the deepest part of her heart. You couldn't hide anything from him. That was what frightened Queenie the most. That was what she tried not to think about. If God could see behind the curtain in her head and into the darkest most secret part of her heart, he would know what she knew. The awful, dreadful truth that she knew the babies were being killed and she did nothing to stop it till the end. She could have saved some of the poor little mites, but instead she bought soap and ribbons and fancy new boots.

She couldn't tell the chaplain that. She couldn't tell anyone that. There was no need, if God already knew. Queenie thought that maybe she should pray. She could pray for the babies that were left and the babies that were gone. But what good would it do now?

'I have nothing to confess,' she kept telling the chaplain. 'I have nothing to say. Only that I am innocent.' The chaplain always sighed heavily at this and left her cell with disappointment in his eyes.

Mam and Da had visited a few times and brought some comforts: a thick blanket, an extra shawl and parcels of bread, cheese and apples. Da was in a terrible way. His eyes were red-rimmed and wild-looking, but there was no whiff of drink about him. He kept holding Queenie to him, but wouldn't say a word.

Mam was better at it all. She talked of what they would do when Queenie came home; about the fine knees-up the lot of them would have with Ellen and Mary and all. She told Queenie how big the new baby had grown, how Da had been off the drink for an age now, and how Tally had been taking himself off to school. She brought Tally in once. He'd grown so handsome. He looked Queenie straight in the eye.

'You ain't done nothing wrong,' he said. 'No matter what they're all saying. I know you ain't done nothing wrong.'

Ellen had been released without charge and came to visit too. Queenie was glad her sister had only had to endure a week in the cells. She was in lodgings now with her baby and Mary, and Queenie was chuffed that Ellen had named the baby after her. Little Queenie. She was doing well, Ellen had told her. Ellen had stayed an hour. It had been hard to know what to say in all that time, so they'd mostly just held hands.

Yesterday, at just before nine in the morning, the bells had rung out for the hanging of Mrs Waters and Mrs Ellis. The crowds outside had been jubilant.

'Hang the murderers. Hang the murderers!' they'd shouted. Queenie had stuffed her fingers in her ears and hummed to drown out the noise.

And now here she was, with one more night left. Tomorrow she'd be in front of the judge at the Old Bailey. Tomorrow she'd know.

She heard the clanking of keys and banging of doors, and the moans and cries of other prisoners. She pulled the blanket tight around her shoulders and tried to imagine herself at home and away from this nowhere place that was neither before nor after. She pictured them all huddled round the fire with hot cheeks and cold toes. Da would be singing and Mam would be smiling and the little ones would be curled up in her skirts. Tomorrow, she promised herself. Tomorrow will be different. And she closed her eyes and wished and wished for some quietness.

*   *   *

Guilty.

A word, just a word.

And then there was silence. Like the air had been sucked from the room; a moment stretched tight. Then slowly, slowly the soft whispering of voices and the rustling of petticoats and skirts and the scratching of pens on paper filtered into the courtroom. Queenie – standing trembling in the dock – felt her knees buckle beneath her and a blackness swam in front of her eyes. A shriek burst from the spectators' gallery. Two officials rushed to the dock and hoisted Queenie to her feet. They slapped her face until she was forced to open her eyes.

Silence again. Then the judge cleared his throat and asked Queenie whether she had anything to say as to why sentence of the law should not be passed upon her.

'Only that I am innocent, sir,' she whispered. The square of black cloth was laid upon the judge's powdered wig and he looked at Queenie solemnly as he spoke the most dreaded words of all.

'The court doth order you to be taken from hence to the place from whence you came, and thence to the place of execution, and that you be hanged by the neck until you are dead, and that your body be afterward buried within the precincts of the prison in which you shall be confined after your conviction. And may the Lord have mercy upon your soul!'

The judge's words sailed over Queenie's head. She

looked up to the spectators' gallery and, as a strange quietness pounded in her ears, she saw Mam, Da, Tally and the little 'uns looking down at her, and she knew she was not alone.

Epilogue

London, 1884

The guests will soon be arriving. I check the clock on the mantelpiece. A quarter to six. I must go out to the hall soon and ready myself to greet everyone.

Tally walks into the room and I smile to see a black curl has escaped his efforts to tidy his hair. 'Come here,' I say. He stands in front of me and I lick my fingers and smooth the errant curl back in place. I step back and look him up and down. In truth, he looks so handsome in his new dinner jacket and silk bow tie that my voice catches in my throat as I brush imaginary dust from his shoulders and say, 'There. You will do.'

He bends and kisses my cheek. 'And you, big sister, look good enough to eat.'

I shrug modestly. 'It is only my old blue silk. But I must admit,' I twirl around in front of him, 'Mary has remodelled it beautifully!'

Tally walks to the sideboard, where there are glasses laid out and bottles of wine and Madeira. He pours two small glasses of Madeira and hands one to me. We turn to look at the back of the room – once a grand drawing room, but now used by our girls and their young ones as a place to meet during the day – at the banner that stretches from one corner of the ceiling to the other.

Happy Anniversary

'It's hard to believe it's been four whole years now,' says Tally. 'To think, Ellen, we started with just one girl and now we have fifteen!'

I turn to him and we clink our glasses together. 'Oh!' I suddenly remember. 'There is a piece in yesterday's *Morning Advertiser* that I meant to show you.' I go to the table under the window where a newspaper is lying next to a vase of pink roses. I pass the newspaper to Tally but he waves it away.

'You read it to me,' he says. 'You know how slow I am.'

I put my glass down, shake out the newspaper and clear my throat.

'The Haven of Hope for Homeless Little Ones,' I begin, reading out loud.

Tomorrow evening the anniversary festival in aid of this institution, which was founded four years ago by Miss Ellen Swift (31) and her brother Mr Tally O'Connor (24) for unmarried mothers and their children, will be held at Castle House, Vine Street, South Westminster.

Miss Swift has in the past made representations to the Royal Commission on the Poor Law about the unsuitability of the workhouse in caring for the unsupported mother and her child. Both she and Mr O'Connor have been relentless in bringing to the attention of the Home

Secretary, the President of the Poor Law and the Chief Commissioner of the Police, the continuation of the dreadful system of baby farming whereby illegitimate children are entrusted into the care of unscrupulous persons who offer to adopt them and bring them up, 'with all a mother's care', for a sum of money, only for the helpless infants to be subjected to a slow and merciless death.

Both Miss Swift and Mr O'Connor were instrumental in the formation of the Infant Life Protection Society, which now operates to oversee the registration and supervision of nurses or baby farmers and the children entrusted into their care. It is hoped that the 'wholesale massacre of infants' which had grown to unprecedented proportions in the capital will continue to decline and the perpetrators of the ghastly crimes be brought to justice.

I finish reading and look at Tally for his reaction. He is silent for a moment, then his usual serious frown turns to a smile.

'We *are* making a difference, ain't we?' he says.

I put the newspaper down and put my hand in his. 'I *know* we are,' I say. 'Our girls know we are, and . . .' I squeeze his hand tightly, 'you can be sure Queenie knows we are too.'

There are noises from the hall. Mary puts her head around the door. 'The first carriages have arrived,' she says, her cheeks flushed with excitement.

A dark head appears behind her, then a pair of startling

green eyes. 'Mother! Hurry!' says Little Queenie. Although these days she prefers to be called plain Queenie, to her constant frustration, we always forget. 'Come on!' she shouts again.

I keep hold of Tally's hand, and together we walk to the hall to meet our guests.

The writing of *The Quietness*:
a note from the author

A few years ago, while researching the dark side of the Victorian era for another book I was writing, I came across the mention of a practice I had never heard of before – baby farming. I dug deeper and was appalled and fascinated by what I learned.

In Victorian England, it was considered the ultimate sin for an unmarried girl or woman to fall pregnant and give birth to an illegitimate child. A single mother was shunned by society and often by her family too. Abortions were illegal and 'back street' abortions dangerous. It was impossible to find work with a child in tow and 'fallen women', as they were labelled, were left with little choice but to throw themselves at the mercy of the workhouse, or to turn to prostitution. But there was a third option.

In most newspapers of the day, if you looked carefully among the miscellaneous advertisement columns – those advertising pieces of furniture for sale or seeking someone to take in washing, for example – you could find coded notices such as 'Child wanted to nurse' or 'Respectable married couple seek care of child'.

These adverts were usually placed by baby farmers, that is, women seeking to adopt illegitimate children for a sum

of money. A baby farmer offered a solution to single pregnant women desperate to avoid shaming themselves and
their families. If a pregnant woman had the means to pay,
she could also rent a room in a 'house of confinement' and
hide away for the duration of her pregnancy. Many baby
farmers offered this service and for an additional fee, they
would keep the newborn baby, allowing the mother to go
back to her life as though nothing had happened.

Most single mothers who handed their child over to a
baby farmer knew they would never see that child again.
The majority of baby farmers looked after the children for
a while before re-homing them or selling them on to child-
less couples. But some baby farmers had a far more sinister
method of getting rid of these unwanted children.

The characters of Margaret Waters and Sarah Ellis are
based on real-life sisters of the same names. They were
known as the 'Brixton Baby Farmers', and between them
were thought to have murdered by starvation at least nine-
teen infants. In 1870 Margaret Waters became the first baby
farmer in England to be hanged for her crimes. Sarah Ellis
was convicted of obtaining money under false pretences
and was sentenced to eighteen months' imprisonment with
hard labour.

I read the original transcript of the trial which took place
at the Old Bailey. One of the witnesses was a young servant
girl who worked for Margaret Waters and Sarah Ellis. I could
hear the girl's voice through the transcribed words and
became fascinated by the life I imagined she led and the
circumstances she lived through. The horror of what went
on inside the baby farm lived with me, alongside the voice

of the servant girl, and I couldn't help wondering what life would have been like for this Victorian teenage girl and whether she had been fully aware of what was going on.

The servant girl was to become the Queenie of this book. Here's an extract from the trial transcript which gave me her voice.

In June last I was employed as a servant by Mrs Waters at 4, Frederick Terrace.

I am getting on for fourteen. There was no other servant in the house besides myself. I did all the housework and used to attend to the children very often. There were about fourteen persons in the house. Mrs Waters, Mrs Ellis, myself and eleven children.

None of them used to cry hardly, they all seemed to be ill. The whole of them. The children used to be laid all day on the sofa up till about six thirty, sometimes seven o'clock. I might hear one of them just begin to cry and I would go and put a teat in its mouth and it would go to sleep again. They were very silent children – nobody ever tried to rouse them. I thought the children were ill – I used to say, 'That child is ill ain't it ma'm?'

Persons used to call at the house sometimes. If anyone knocked at the door with a double knock I was to take the children into another room. She said she would not get another child if they heard the children crying. I always did so when they came – sometimes there would be one a day – someone would come perhaps and knock a double knock, and then we would take the children into another room before we undid the door.

The children that were taken away used to be washed in the morning, and sometimes their faces were sponged when they were taken out. They looked very ill when they went away. Mrs Waters used to say she was taking them home to their parents or to a better home in the country.

I don't know what became of the servant girl. I'd love to find out. Did she know what was happening, or not? Maybe I'll look her up on the census one day. I do wonder though, what she would have thought of being the inspiration for a book written nearly one hundred and fifty years later.